# GIRLS DON'T FLY

### Kristen Chandler

**VIKING**

An Imprint of Penguin Group (USA) Inc.

VIKING
Published by Penguin Group
Penguin Group (USA) Inc., 345 Hudson Street, New York, New York 10014, U.S.A.
Penguin Group (Canada), 90 Eglinton Avenue East, Suite 700, Toronto, Ontario, Canada M4P 2Y3
(a division of Pearson Penguin Canada Inc.)
Penguin Books Ltd, 80 Strand, London WC2R 0RL, England
Penguin Ireland, 25 St Stephen's Green, Dublin 2, Ireland (a division of Penguin Books Ltd)
Penguin Group (Australia), 250 Camberwell Road, Camberwell, Victoria 3124, Australia
(a division of Pearson Australia Group Pty Ltd)
Penguin Books India Pvt Ltd, 11 Community Centre, Panchsheel Park, New Delhi – 110 017, India
Penguin Group (NZ), 67 Apollo Drive, Rosedale, Auckland 0632, New Zealand
(a division of Pearson New Zealand Ltd.)
Penguin Books (South Africa) (Pty) Ltd, 24 Sturdee Avenue, Rosebank, Johannesburg 2196, South Africa

Penguin Books Ltd, Registered Offices: 80 Strand, London WC2R 0RL, England

First published in 2011 by Viking, a member of Penguin Group (USA) Inc.

1   3   5   7   9   10   8   6   4   2

Copyright © Kristen Chandler, 2011
All rights reserved

LIBRARY OF CONGRESS CATALOGING-IN-PUBLICATION DATA
Chandler, Kristen.
Girls don't fly / by Kristen Chandler.
p. cm.
Summary: Myra, a high school senior, will do almost anything to win a contest and earn money
for a study trip to the Galápagos Islands, which would mean getting away from her demanding
family life in Utah and ex-boyfriend Erik, but Erik is set on winning the same contest.
ISBN 978-0-670-01331-9 (hardcover)
[1. Family life—Utah—Fiction. 2. Scholarships—Fiction. 3. Contests—Fiction.
4. Dating (Social customs)—Fiction. 5. Pregnancy—Fiction. 6. Galápagos Islands—Fiction.
7. Utah—Fiction.] I. Title. II. Title: Girls do not fly.
PZ7.C359625Gir 2011        [Fic]—dc22        2011010563

Printed in U.S.A.        Set in Berkeley        Book design by Nancy Brennan

*To Jessie,*
*who flew*

~~~~~~~~~~

# 1

# Habitat:
*The place where you're stuck.*

If I close my eyes and concentrate on the squawking gulls and the heat of the sun on my skin, it's almost like I'm at the beach. With Erik. I breathe deeply the salty air coming off the waves. I'm toasted brown and relaxed in my swimsuit. Erik has his fingers woven into mine, but we're not sweaty, itchy, or about to talk about our relationship. I'm not afraid of anything and nothing is ever going to change, because this moment is absolutely perfect.

If I open my eyes, I'm still living in Landon. The pit of Utah.

I keep my eyes shut as long as I can.

"Myra?" yells Carson.

I sit up fast. My six-year-old brother stands in front of me. His face is streaked with mud. "He's dead."

I get to my feet. "Who?"

"Spinosaurus. He's disappeared."

I survey our beat yard. Andrew and Brett are building a fort out of a packing box and for the time being they aren't hitting each other. I say, "Maybe he's just growing up to be a fossil."

Carson drops his head. "He's too young to be a fossil."

I take Carson's muddy fingers out of his mouth and swab him with a tissue I keep in my pocket. "We'll find him. It's okay."

The gulls bellyache overhead. Carson says, "The birds got him."

"No. Gulls don't like dinosaurs," I say.

Carson says, "I don't like seagulls."

I like seagulls. These are from the Great Salt Lake, which is about ten miles from my house. Everyone thinks of them as trash birds, but not every bird would pick a field clean of crickets for starving pioneers. The Mormons say God got the birds to do it, but God or no God, seagulls have been cleaning up ever since.

Over by the house, my parents pretend to discuss patio cement, my mother's latest home improvement project. Their unhappy voices drift across the yard. "If you settle for something you don't want, you live to regret it," says Mom, shifting my youngest brother to her other hip. She's hauled six of us around on those hips, but Danny's way too big for her to be packing.

Dad rubs his forehead. "Sometimes you just have to make the best of things."

"And sometimes you have to cut your losses," Mom chirps.

This conversation is actually about my previously perfect sister, Melyssa. She and Zeke are coming over to talk about their wedding plans, but she's late. About five months late. One year into her full ride to college and my genius sister couldn't figure out how not to get pregnant. My parents have been out of their minds since they found out two weeks ago.

"And what do you suggest?" says Dad.

Mom says, "As if what *I suggest* matters."

"I want to play," says Danny.

Mom carts Danny back into the shadow of the house. Dad stands looking around for a minute and then follows her in. I should rescue Danny, but I know my mom needs something to hold on to this afternoon.

In a few minutes I find Carson's missing toy dinosaur and order is restored to the universe. I go back to my plastic chair. It's only the end of February and the snow's already gone. I'm hoping for a sunburn before my date with Erik tonight. I have absolutely no idea what to wear. He said he wants to take me "someplace nice," which could be a good thing, but what if it isn't?

I close my eyes again and listen to the gulls' high-pitched cries. They always sound so much better when they're flying than when they're on the ground, like the wind gives them a different vocabulary. I slip off my shoes. When I close my eyes this time I still see Erik with his shirt off, but there's no water or birds or hand-holding. It's not perfect either.

I open my eyes. More gulls. Not peaceful, soaring gulls, but a squadron of big white bombers headed right for our yard. Squawking like crazy. Coming in for a landing. Dive-bombing on a patch of spilled cheese crackers. Andrew and Brett pick up rocks before the first bird touches ground.

"Leave them alone," I call over the screeching.

Not even the birds look up.

I yell louder, "Don't. Even. Think. About it."

I run across the dirt in my bare feet and catch Andrew's hand.

"Get 'em!" yells Andrew.

The birds flutter but don't fly. Brett takes aim and I reach for his hand too. Brett brings his arm down to get away and hits me square in the eye with his rock. It rings my bell all the way down.

"Wow, sorry, Myra," says Brett.

"The rock," I say, sucking air. The second thing I think about, after how I probably have brain damage, is that I'm going to look like a prizefighter at dinner tonight.

Brett says, "Are you okay?"

The birds fly. I feel dizzy. I get back to my chair and sit down. The boys follow me.

"Sorry. But why d'ya always have to do that?" says Andrew. "They're trash birds."

That's just how it goes, I guess—if you clean up after someone they think you're the garbage. "We don't throw rocks at birds."

Carson wails, "You're bleeding."

I rub my face. Even my eyelashes hurt. I have a streak of

blood on my hand. It's small, but I shiver. I don't do blood. Too many germs. Brett stares at me, not moving. I know he's freaked out because he's not even trying to blame Andrew. "I'm fine," I say. "It's a long ways from my heart." That's what we always say when someone gets hurt in my family.

"Go back and play."

Brett says, "I didn't mean to."

A stray gull flies back into the yard and begins pecking for crumbs. The boys look at the bird and then at me. Their hands hang at their sides, fingers twitching.

I glare at them with my bloody eye. They shrug off to the fort.

I walk over to the bird to scare it away. I finally have to kick at it to make it fly. Some birds are just too dumb to know when it's time to go.

My eye is already starting to swell. I head to the house for ice. I try to think positively about tonight. Maybe someplace nice really is nice. Why am I so worried? People who care about each other cut the other person some slack, right? Right.

Melyssa's junker chugs into the front yard. I don't want to go inside now, but I have to if I want to get the ice.

I know where someplace nice is. Someplace else.

# Brood Parasites:

*When a bird stows its eggs or other junk*
*in another bird's nest.*

"Wow," says Dad as I walk in. He's looking at Melyssa, who is eating a sandwich the size of her head. And believe me, for such a small person, she has a big head.

Melyssa says, "Yeah, I'm not one bit sick."

"She can eat," says Zeke.

"Shut up, Zeke."

Zeke laughs. "She tried to eat the mailman yesterday. Had to hit her with a stick a few times to get his leg out of her mouth."

Melyssa and Zeke smile at each other. Zeke looks like the Incredible Hulk next to Mel. He's square and stands like a wrestler, which is funny for a poet. He's also the only guy Mel's ever dated who's as mean as she is, so I guess they're perfect for each other. I mean I like Zeke, he's funny and whatever, but I wish Melyssa wasn't pregnant and I wish Zeke didn't smell like old cheese. But then, I wish a lot of things.

"What do you need?" says Mom, not looking at me. I'm not invited to this conversation. Biologically, I'm eighteen months younger than my sister, but in mom-years I'm permanently at the little kids' table.

"I need ice," I say.

"What did you do to yourself?" says Melyssa.

Mom just shakes her head. "I've told you about letting those boys play so rough with you. You don't need a doctor, do you?"

"No. I'll be fine."

The boys follow me into the kitchen. Danny jumps out of my mother's lap and runs for my legs. The other three start for the kitchen cupboard.

"Could you take the mob to their rooms then?" says Mom. This whole thing with Melyssa has bankrupted her patience reserves.

I herd the mob down the hallway.

Andrew says, "They're eating. Why can't we eat?"

"Melyssa's going to get fat, isn't she?" says Brett.

Melyssa inherited my mother's metabolism, which is to say she could give birth to an ice-cream truck and not gain weight. Danny takes my hand. He's four, but he's not much of a talker.

Carson, who never stops talking, takes my other hand. "Dinosaurs are eating my stomach out."

"Clean off and then go wait for me in your room."

Brett says, "Why do they always get rid of us? It's not like we don't know how you make a baby."

"How do you make a baby?" says Carson.

I glare at Brett. He's eleven and trouble, but in a fight I'd want him on my side.

Andrew, our twelve-year-old hall monitor, says, "Are they going to move here? I don't want to sleep in the basement."

I sigh. "*You'll* get *your* room."

"Then where will you sleep?" says Carson.

I wonder if people still stow away on ships. I'm tall but I compress well. "You can't put a new baby in an unfinished basement."

"Sucks to be you," says Brett.

"Don't say 'sucks.'" I push my brothers into the bathroom. "Soap. And hang up your towels."

"We're not babies," says Andrew.

"No, you're a whole lot messier."

I head back for the kitchen. No one talks while I slather around the peanut butter. Dad fills a washcloth with ice and hands it to me as I walk out of the kitchen. "They beat you up pretty good."

"Long ways from my heart," I say, imitating him. He grimaces. I do a perfect impression of my dad.

I walk slowly down the hall so I can eavesdrop. I put the cloth to my eye and the ice makes it stick to my skin. In the kitchen there is a brief back and forth and then I hear Dad say, "I'm sorry . . . but I just can't believe you'd be so irresponsible. How will you make this work? And what about this family? You've just proved to every person in this community that they were right about us. Those godless Morgans . . .”

Melyssa yells, “Half the girls I knew in high school got knocked up. And I don't even live here anymore.”

“Well, we do,” says Dad. “When you're management, these kinds of things matter. Having people's respect pays your bills, young lady.”

Mel says, “I'm not a lady now, remember.”

“Oh please!” Mom explodes.

I hear another explosive sound, this time from the boys' room. Mom's high-pitched voice slices down the hall. “Myra!”

I hustle to the boys' room with the sandwiches. There is broken glass all over the floor and Carson is yelling, “911! 911!” They all have bare feet so I make everyone mount their beds and toss them their rations. If I try to evacuate there will be blood.

I point at them individually. “Don't move.”

“Brett did it,” yells Carson.

Brett squints at him but says nothing. He's plotting.

“I'm not getting on the bed,” says Andrew.

“'Cause he's so mature,” says Brett.

“Shut up.”

“You shut up.”

I leave them to torment each other while I jog down the hall and grab a broom and garbage can. The phone rings.

I drop the broom and run for the phone. I can always tell when it's Erik, sometimes even before the phone rings. I let out a breath before I answer. “Hello.”

"Hey, Myra." I can barely hear Erik's tenor voice over the boys' yelling. "It sounds like somebody's getting killed over there."

"My brothers are mud wrestling."

"Really?"

"Um . . . no."

He pauses and then laughs. "Okay. So how are you?" He sounds happy, normal.

"Great," I say.

"Good. Good. Hey, well, I have a problem with tonight."

"Okay . . . like what?" I don't even try to sound happy.

"Can I meet you . . . like, right now? I could come get you in about ten minutes."

I look around at the eight levels of chaos in my house. "Let me check."

I walk into the kitchen. "Can I go meet Erik for a few minutes?" No one answers.

I say, "I'll sweep the glass up and then put on a movie for the boys."

Mom points her tiny finger at me. "I don't need you running off with a boy right now."

Two weeks of this. Like the world has come to an end. Like somewhere in China they're having updates in Tiananmen Square about the Morgan Family Illegitimate Pregnancy Crisis. "*I'm* not running off." It slips out.

Melyssa shoots me a death glare.

My mother shakes her head again and turns back to her

important daughter. Okay, maybe she's not more important, but she and Mom have always just gotten along better. Mom and I are too alike, in all the wrong ways. Dad gives me the mercy nod. It means I don't have to listen to Mom as long as I don't argue with her.

I go back to the phone. The boys are jumping on the beds, into the walls, making loud thumping sounds. I take another breath. "Hey. Ten minutes is fine. And I have a funny-looking eye."

"Oh . . ." Erik says. "Why?"

"I got in the middle of something."

"Huh," says Erik. "Is it bad?"

I press the swelling lid. "It's gonna get ugly, but I'll live."

# 3

# Drift Migration:

*When birds get dumped on by the weather
and then get seriously lost.*

Erik drives up in his white truck exactly ten minutes later. When I answer the door everything else disappears. He's wearing my favorite pale yellow shirt. His spiky black hair is messed up from driving with his window down. Just opening the door with him on the other side makes me relax and get excited all at the same time. He looks startled by my black eye, but he grins anyway. That smile cleans my head of every other messy thought.

He's holding daisies wrapped in fuchsia cellophane and tied with a silk bow. Daisies. He says, "I thought you'd like these."

"Are you crazy!" I say. "I love them." I feel ridiculous. It's going to be fine. I imagined how distant he's been. Okay, I didn't imagine it. But at least it's over.

He opens his mouth. Only air comes out. When Erik is nervous he forgets how to talk. We both do that. I love that we have the same quirks.

"Let me put these away, okay," I say. *Breathe,* I tell myself. *See, everything is fine.* I walk into the kitchen and grab a vase without looking at anyone. I don't want anything in the kitchen to touch me.

Dad says, "Those are nice."

"Half an hour," says Mom. "We've got a lot to do today."

Zeke says, "That kid's making me look bad."

"He's Prince Charming," Mel says. The edge to her voice cuts in all directions. "But who makes you look good?"

Erik and I walk into the front yard. The lawn is too wet to sit down on, so we sit at the bottom of the porch steps. "Melyssa and Zeke are here. My parents are still losing it."

Erik pushes my bangs out of my eyes. "Your eye looks hot. How'd you get it?"

"Stopping a fight between Andrew and Brett and a seagull."

"Your brothers were fighting a bird?"

"They were going to kill it with rocks."

"So you saved the bird with your face," he says. "That's so you." Erik looks at me funny. He smiles and reaches out for my hand. His hands are soft and familiar. I tell myself to stop worrying. He brought me flowers. For all I know he's about to ask me to Senior Dinner Dance. It's not until May, but Erik likes to plan. Everyone thinks he's so cocky because he's smart and good at track, but they don't see how he worries about stuff. Like me.

I say, "I'm sorry . . . I've been such a mess."

"Yeah . . . but it's not like it's your fault."

"I cried mascara on your jacket in front of half the track team."

"My mom got it out."

He takes a deep breath. He's always telling me to do that. Maybe because he had asthma when he was a kid, which is another thing most people don't know about Erik. "Can we go for a drive?"

The distance between us is back again, like a persistent draft. "I better not. My parents need me to keep one 'eye' on the boys this morning." I point at my shiner but he doesn't laugh.

Finally I say, "So . . . what are the flowers for?"

Erik lets air out of his mouth like a tire. Then he takes another deep breath and does the whole thing again. This is bad. Finally he says, "I want to break up."

It takes a few seconds for me to hear what he said.

"You brought me daisies . . . to break up with me?"

He swivels like his pale yellow shirt doesn't fit. "I'm sorry. I just need some space."

"Space?" The word comes up in my mouth.

"We can still go out, once in a while."

"Once in a while?"

"You know, until school gets out."

"Until school gets out?"

"You're repeating things."

"I am?"

I am. I've dated Erik for nineteen months. We met in Foods and Nutrition. He said I whipped egg whites like a gourmet. I liked how he held the door for girls, no matter what they looked like, and how he always remembered to wash his hands before we started cooking.

"Are you okay?" he says.

How could I be okay?

On our first date we made a fire in the canyon and charred marshmallows. On our second date we went downtown to a sandwich shop with pool tables and he hummed in my ear while he showed me how to hold my cue. On our third date he brought me daisies for the first time and I got grounded because we stayed out past midnight talking about him wanting to be a dentist like his dad even though everyone thinks it's all because of the money and of course it isn't because Erik isn't like that. For Christmas he gave me a necklace with a white pearl the size of a grape, and a note that said, "For a treasure."

"Why?" I say.

"Why what?"

"Why do you need more space?" I know this is a pathetic question, by the way. But it wasn't exactly space he wanted the other night.

He holds his palms up and looks at them. Then he opens up his mouth and air comes out again.

"I don't give you space?"

"Sure. But we're going to graduate in three and a half months . . ." he says, like I might not know. "I'm going to be gone a lot. And then college . . ."

His palms get interesting again. We look at his hands together. I know his hands better than my own.

I unhook the chain dangling a pearl from my neck and feel like I have torn the seam that holds my life together. "Here."

He puts out his hand. "Myra . . . you don't have to give that back."

I drop the pearl in his hand.

"We can still hang out." He stands up to leave and puts the necklace in his shirt pocket.

I stand up too. I don't want to be sitting down when he leaves.

I watch his truck drive away. I don't cry. But I sit back down. I hurt everywhere. My skin doesn't fit. I want to disappear but I can't. I can't do anything. Except take up space. I stay there until my sister nearly tramples me when she marches out of the house with Zeke.

"Myra. What are you doing out here?"

I don't have any words.

She pats me on the shoulder. "Where's Prince Charming?"

I take her hand off my shoulder. "Someplace else."

# 4

# Torpor:
*When birds freeze up to keep from dying.*

The next morning, after I've tried in vain to die in my sleep, I tell my parents about Erik. They don't take it well. They liked the idea of me being with Erik too. He's the Pre-Dental Golden Boy, or at least he was until he dumped me.

"Where does that kid get off?" says Dad for the third time.

Carson is sitting in the next room watching cartoons, but he comes in when they raise their voices. "Stop yelling at Myra," he says. He comes over and puts his hand on my forehead.

"They aren't yelling *at* me," I tell him. "They're yelling *to* me."

"It's still loud," says Carson. He gets my hand. "Come watch cartoons."

Mom puts her hand stiffly on my shoulder. She looks like she's going to say something, but she just pats my arm.

~~~~~~

I sit next to Carson and watch the grainy reruns of the road-runner outsmarting the coyote, but I end up back in my room with the covers over my head. I don't know who thought up the term "heartache," but they must not have been too bad off if it was only their heart. Everything is burning from the in-side and stabbing from the outside. The sheets feel like they're made of yak hair. The smell of my body under the blanket suffocates me. The more still my body gets the faster my thoughts chase, until I don't think of anything at all except I wish I could stop thinking.

At three o'clock I have to go to work at the Lucky Penny Ice Cream Parlor. Fortunately for me, it's Sunday. I always work Sunday because the religious kids in town aren't supposed to, including Erik. Of course the religious kids come and buy ice cream on Sunday, at least the wicked ones, and when they do I'm there to serve them. So I guess that kind of makes me the devil of ice cream.

I walk to work. On Sundays I usually drive our family's prehistoric Suburban, Moby, but today I need to be outside. The sidewalk goes under me. I see my feet and the cement and the brown water in the canal, but it's like I don't. It's like I don't see anything.

No, that's not true. I see the night last March when Erik dressed up as an Easter bunny to invite me to the junior prom, the time when he wrote, "You're hot!" in chalk on my side-walk for the Fourth of July, and the night he said he thought we should make "a long-term plan." I see that stuff just fine.

I watch the dark water going into the covered tunnel of the canal. I remember last June when Erik took me to a trestle on the Jordan River, south of town. It was early June and we'd had a long winter. The water was dark and high from melting snow. I took one look off that bridge and shook my head. "No way," I said.

He said, "The guys are going to die. I am so getting that penguin."

"The guys" were the track team. The "penguin" is the award they give for the best death dive of the summer. They had said we wouldn't do it, so of course we had to. That's Erik.

"Just hold my hand," he'd said. "You've got this."

I didn't want to, but I didn't want to let him down. When I hit the water I thought my neck was going to snap. The runoff water was like cement, it was so cold. I couldn't breathe or find my feet. Just green, spinning water.

I lost hold of Erik the minute we hit. I was terrified. Sticks hit me and something bigger. I couldn't get right-side up because the current was pushing me down and forward too fast. Then I felt him grab me. I came up. Once I got air I could swim, and then I stumbled to shore.

Erik shook the water from his dark hair. "That was *crazy!*" he yelled.

It was crazy. But when it was over and we weren't dead it seemed like we were heroes. We went out for pizza with his friends that night and they gave us the penguin and sang to us and made me feel like Jane of the Jungle. That was the thing about Erik. He pushed me to try things. Sometimes he pushed too hard. But he pushed me. Now all he wants is to push me away.

When I get to work Callie Kendall is already there. Callie is what you might call an energetic employee, if she's on her meds. If she's off her meds, which happens about once or twice a month depending on whether her family can afford them, she doesn't do too well.

She points at my eye. "What happened to you?"

"My little brother. It was an accident."

"Musta hit you hard. You look like you've had chemo."

Callie's mom has had chemo and Callie talks about it a lot, which is fine. If my mom was having chemo I probably wouldn't talk at all.

I say, "Erik dumped me."

Callie's mouth drops open. "Shut. Up."

I sit down next to her. She smells like hand sanitizer and cigarettes.

"But you're the Dream Team. You're sweet and poor and he's hot and rich." She whistles through her teeth. "Sheez."

"He needs space." I know I shouldn't tell anyone these things, but my defenses are not what they were a few days ago.

"Are you pissed?"

I think about my mom and dad bashing Erik for the past five hours. "No."

"You want me to fix you a shake or something? Maybe we could get him fired. Or key his truck. Or poison him with wild mushrooms. I saw that on TV and they totally couldn't tell until the end when the girl confessed."

"I need to clean something." Some girls get even. I clean.

"The girls' bathroom is trashed," she says.

We walk to the back, where Howard is bringing tubs out of the big freezer. Howard is the manager, and he hates his job, his wife, everyone who works here, and all children. As far as I know the only thing that Howard loves is money, complaining about employees, and experimenting with the boundaries of sexual harassment.

"Outta my way," he huffs as he passes.

Callie says, "Sure thing, boss." And before he can even put the ice cream down Callie says, "Erik dumped Myra."

Howard drops the ice cream and lets out a sweaty grunt. He rubs his jowls with the back of his hand. "Is that right, Myra? Prince Charming gave you the boot?"

"Yesterday," says Callie. "You should fire him. Myra's your best worker."

I shove Callie. "Can I clean tonight if it doesn't get busy?"

"I could fire him," says Howard. "But I'd need a little incentive."

I go with the idea that he's kidding and try to smile. Even trying to try to smile feels awful.

"Is it the Wence girl?" says Howard. "She was in here three nights ago and looked like she was ready to go. I heard she left him a ten-dollar tip."

"Ariel?" says Callie squinting. "Ohmygosh. Ariel?" Then she looks at me. "I mean, she's totally hideous."

The name stops me cold. Ariel is a tall redhead on the

track team with Erik. She has a giant ego and an even bigger overbite, which she thinks makes her look glamorous. How could he date a girl with such bad teeth?

"Don't take it so hard, honey," says Howard. "He's headed for college. You've got great legs. And you shine up a stockroom like nobody's business. Another knucklehead will come along."

Normally I would just ignore Howard. But it's like my head's too thin to hold any water. It just starts springing out of my face like it did last night.

I run to the bathroom and throw up, even though I haven't eaten since yesterday morning. It smells like rotten eggs. I throw up again.

When I'm done, Callie brings me cleanser and the mop.

"My mom does this a lot too," she says.

I wipe my mouth off with some toilet paper. "I'm sorry. . . . How's your mom doing this week?"

"She's bowling tonight," says Callie. "Don't sweat it."

"I'm actually just sweating. But I'm glad she's feeling better."

"You really were sweet together," says Callie. "I'm sorry."

I start my therapy by cleaning the floors. If I pace myself, I ought to be able to keep cleaning until I starve to death or keel over from the fumes of the ammonia cleanser, whichever comes first. Either way this is going to be one heartbreakingly clean bathroom when I'm finished.

# 5

# Vocalization:

*How birds talk to each other.*

Melyssa calls from her apartment when I get home from work. "Hey," she says. "Is Mom there?"

"She's at work. They had a flood in one of the basements."

"So when will she be home?" Her voice is smaller than usual.

"Do you want to talk to Dad? He's out working on the patio."

She sighs. "No, it's okay."

Now that she's sighed I have to ask what's going on. "You don't sound too good."

She sighs again. "Turns out I'm getting sick after all. You wouldn't believe it."

I think of me hunched over the toilet at work. "I might," I say.

"Hey, no. By the way, don't worry about Prince Charming. You weren't serious about him, right?"

"We dated for almost two years," I say.

"He's an idiot."

"Actually, he has a 4.0."

"Yeah. But he's a cocky pretty boy."

I can count on one hand the times that Melyssa has ever even tried to talk to Erik.

She says, "You can't trust a guy who spends more time ironing his shirts than you do."

"His mom irons his shirts," I say.

Mel keeps talking. "Even worse. Trust me. He gels his hair to look messy."

"I like his hair. And he's not cocky, he's just smart. He's going to be a dentist."

"A dentist? Please. Myra, how boring."

There's a miserable silence that I hope Mel knows is her fault. She says, "Well, at least he showers. I mean Zeke showers, just not regularly. I'm trying to help you not be a door-mat."

I say, "I'm a *doormat* now? Because I like clean clothes and hair?"

"No, you've always been a doormat."

I feel like I did when Brett hit me in the eye, but this doesn't just ring my bell, it cracks it.

"You really think I'm a *doormat*?"

"Come on, Myra. You're a compulsive pleaser. You try to make ev-er-y-body happy."

"What's so wrong with that?"

"Nothing. Except that you can't do it and people will treat you like crap. Other than that it's pretty cool."

I try to breathe. Erik is (was) always reminding me to breathe. I say, "Why did you call?"

"Just wanted to help."

"I feel so much better."

"Fine. But there's a lot more like him, believe me."

"There isn't anyone like him," I say. And then I put the receiver back in the holder. I don't slam it down. I put it down politely. Doormats are like that. We like to keep the dirt under our rugs.

# 6

# Irruption:

*When a bird shows up where it doesn't normally go.*

Erik and I have only one class together this semester. Advanced Placement biology. Before you get the wrong idea about me I can explain. I'm the invisible student. I get good grades because I take easy classes and I hand everything in on time. I don't talk in class. Most of my teachers have no idea who I am and that's just fine with me. I like science, but I took the AP biology class because it fit in my schedule and because Erik is taking it and because, well, just because.

I've been planning to skip AP bio since three o'clock this morning. But I go. I'm not much of a sluffer. I sit in the back, next to Jonathon Hempilmeyer. There's always a seat next to Jonathon because he can't talk about anything but his horror movies and he has a big, germy nose ring. I actually kind of like Jonathon, except for the nose thing.

"How come you're sitting by me today?" he says.

I stare blankly for a second. He probably knows I've been dumped, but I like to think that maybe he doesn't. I attempt perkiness. "So do you make real movies, or just stuff with your phone?"

"Why, do you want to be in one?"

I laugh. "Just curious. What are they about?"

Jonathon's nose ring wiggles when he talks. "Your black eye is cool. How do you feel about eviscerated intestines?"

Erik comes in. He avoids looking at me and of course I don't look at him because I'm asking Jonathon an important question.

"What about intestines?"

"That's my movie. It's called *Sausage Girls*. Sixty minutes and you'll never be the same."

I hear Erik ask the girl in the tight T-shirt next to him for a pencil. She's delighted to give it to him.

Ms. Miller stands at the front of class in her white lab coat. She's always in a lab coat, no matter what we're doing in class. Ms. Miller says, "Today we're having a guest speaker. . . ."

What I like about Ms. Miller is that she explains things without making fun of students. What I don't like about her is that she always looks depressed when she hands back our tests, like we've personally disappointed her.

Suddenly Jonathon leans over to me and whispers, "Did you break up with Erik?"

I should have taken the seat by Alicia Smelinich.

Jonathon's nose ring is tinkling with excitement. "No more Dream Team? Seriously?"

I keep my eyes glued on Ms. Miller and the guy at the front in the rumpled brown clothes.

Jonathon whispers, "Really?"

I look at Jonathon. I'm expecting him to be appropriately jaded. But instead his eyes are wide, like I just broke the news about the tooth fairy.

He says, "I mean he's kind of uptight, but you two just seemed like you were perfect. You're kind of wreckin' my day here."

I scoot in my chair so I don't have to listen. Jonathon makes movies about body parts. He's supposed to hate Dream Team romances.

"So what happened?" he whispers. "Did he cheat on you?"

I look ahead like I don't hear him.

"It's not like you aren't smokin' hot."

If he keeps talking I swear I'm going to whack my face into the desk.

Ms. Miller says, "This is Peter Tree. He's a graduate student at the University of Utah who specializes in evolutionary biology. He's here to tell us about a project the university is sponsoring in this school district. I'd appreciate all of you giving him your undivided attention. That includes Myra and Jonathon."

Everyone except Erik turns and looks at me—in case anyone hadn't noticed I wasn't next to Erik. Instead I'm next to Jonathon, getting busted by Ms. Miller.

"Okay," says the biology guy with this low, serious voice,

like he's on the radio. He's twentysomething, with longish red-brown hair and a scruffy beard, and he's underfed, like he's been on one too many campouts. But his eyes remind me of Carson's. "What can anyone tell me about the Galápagos Islands?"

For a second everyone does a double take. The Galápagos what?

The biology guy unfolds a giant map and hangs it on the blackboard. There is a red circle around some little tiny islands out in the middle of the ocean next to Ecuador.

Biology guy, who clearly is missing a few screws, flips into this weird Einstein voice and points out the red circle. "Here are the Galápagos Islands," he says.

After a moment of silence a few hyperachievers raise their hands. Of course the weird biology guy calls on Erik.

"They're the islands that Darwin visited when he invented evolution."

The biology guy goes back to being a grown-up. "Well, Darwin didn't invent evolution. But he did write a very famous theory about evolution, using what he observed on the Galápagos Islands."

Erik looks bugged, maybe even embarrassed. Like I say, Erik's not as cocky as people think.

"So I'm here today to tell you about a program that will allow two high school seniors from this school district to travel to the Galápagos Islands for eight weeks this summer with our research team to study plant and bird life. We have been given a generous endowment from an anonymous donor to help pay for some less advantaged students to go learn about evolution, hands-on."

"Less advantaged? What's that supposed to mean?" says Erik.

Ms. Miller steps in front of the class. "What Mr. Tree is trying to say is that this school district has been notably lacking in its science scores. Some people at the university would like to help turn that around."

"By sending us to an island?" Jonathon says. "When should I pack?"

"You might want to read the fine print first," says the biology guy. "Candidates have to attend a ten-week prep class held on Saturday mornings at the Great Salt Lake Marina and then write a research proposal. We roll at six a.m. sharp." The whole class groans on cue. The biology guy just smiles. "Then applicants are selected on the basis of the proposal, just like research fellows are given money for grants based on the fertility of their studies."

"You have to be fertile to win?" says the tight shirt next to Erik.

Obviously the biology guy's not used to talking to high school students. Over the laughing he says, "You choose something you'd like to study there and explain why it's important, and then make a proposal explaining your objective. Fertility is optional."

Ms. Miller says, "It's a scholarship program." Which is a boring enough way of putting it that we all stop laughing.

Peter Tree drops his voice another octave. "But like I was saying, the trip is subsidized, not completely funded by the school. You need to raise one thousand dollars. But the upside is you get college credit for the eight weeks in paradise." He makes a face like a ghoul. "Those are the provisions of the donor."

Whatever, weird biology guy. Wrong school. I wonder what the moneybags donor was thinking. If he or she wanted to "advantage us," he or she should have figured we wouldn't be lying around in money.

"What kind of fund-raising?" asks Alicia Smelinich. "Like selling cookie dough or something?"

"That'd be a lot of cookie dough." The biology guy laughs. "But I suppose you could do it that way. There aren't a lot of rules about the fund-raising, since this is the first year. You just have to have the money before you submit your project on May first. The trip is in July."

"May is less than three months," says Jonathon.

"Eighty-three dollars a week," says Erik.

"It's a lot to ask, I know," says the biology guy. "But it's also a great opportunity."

"So Mr. Tree, could we just have our parents come up with the money?" says David Marquez from the other side of the room. His parents both work at General Cooper and are about as likely to come up with the money as they are to give away gold bullion at Halloween.

"The foundation hopes the students will raise their own funds, but they don't require it."

A thousand dollars for a science trip? Obviously he isn't talking to us. Kids around here don't just pull that kind of money out of their pockets. Except Erik. He's sitting there like he's just found five aces in his deck. And why not? His dad makes that much money before lunch every day.

A year ago I could have covered the whole thing, but that was before I started trying to dress like Erik's friends and I wrecked Moby while backing out of the grocery store parking lot. Now I have a grand total of two hundred and thirteen dollars in my bank account, and six neatly ironed ones in my wallet.

The biology guy says, "So anyway, here's a little video about the trip. In case you're curious. And even if you aren't, the video shows you a little about the islands and why they're so important. Plus, they're hot. Literally."

A few people laugh again. Mostly people start talking about other stuff, like what a weirdo this guy is.

"Class," says Ms. Miller. "Let's be quiet so we can watch the movie."

Jonathon leans over to me. I can see a speck of brown on his teeth. "A thousand bucks? Yeah. That's fair."

I nod. Since when did fair have anything to do with anything? At least it's going to be dark for a few minutes and I can drift off into my own torture chamber while Erik plans his next great adventure. Too bad he and Tight Shirt can't win the competition together so he could borrow her pencil, or whatever, for the whole two months.

Ms. Miller's voice slices through the room. "Class, you may now shut up."

Everyone goes silent.

The movie starts off with drums and a smoking volcano and then flashes to seething waves and black lava beds, then to mangrove forests, ocean caverns, and fog-fringed mountain peaks. The narrator says something about the islands being a microcosm for the earth's development. I put my head down on my desk.

Jonathon bumps me. "Check it out."

I lift my head up. In spite of wanting to dissolve into a puddle I can't help but watch. The water is so blue. One of the blue-footed boobies nearly flies into the camera. Its aqua feet scale over rocks. I hear Erik say, "Get out! Wouldn't you love to go there?"

His new buddy giggles. "Oh, sure."

I stare at the movie. I'm having a hard time swallowing. I tell myself to breathe. I think about Erik going to this place while I stay here and rot, and then I have to concentrate on the movie to keep from totally losing it.

After a minute or two I let the music and the panoramic ocean shots wash over me. It's hard not to. Not only is the water amazingly, perfectly blue, the sky is perfectly pink. The rocks are perfectly jagged. The tortoises are perfectly old. The sea lions are perfectly playful. Even the scientist leading the expedition looks perfect in her little explorer gear.

The narrator says something about "the cruel but essential

element of change." The scientist lady talks about how the islands were born from violent changes in the earth's core and now everything from the albatross to the algae exists largely because of these changes. And for some weird, deeply self-absorbed reason, the longer I watch, the more this is all freakishly interesting to me.

I'm probably just feeling insane, but before I know what is happening to me I'm bonding with every lizard and lava rock. My brain is swallowing seawater. The scientist says something about it being a place that is new geologically, because of all the volcanic activity. It's like a younger miniversion of the earth. Its isolation makes it uniquely suited to Darwin's discoveries and all the other discoveries that have come after. The narrator butts in and says, "It's a place where we can study the birth of things, and a place where animal and plant life can teach us secrets about all life. One cannot help but feel that this is a place to begin."

The camera shows a marine iguana hurling itself off the rocks into the sea to find food. His thick shadow disappears into the water, where he's thrown against the razor coral. Sea lions harass him. The tide flips him in all directions.

I look over at Jonathon. He's sound asleep.

For twenty more minutes I listen to the scientist talk about her impressions of this place. She visits cavernous holes in the earth and ambles up mountains shooting from the sea. In her lovely Texas twang she says, "Thanks to the isolation of these islands and the high rate of volcanic activity, so much about the archipelago is relatively pristine, and yet changing at a faster rate than places with less tectonic convergence. To study this special place is like studying time-lapse photography of creation itself."

I'm not sure I understand what she just said, but I love how it sounds. Everyone in the film is smart and brown and far from here, especially the scientist. I bet she never sucked anybody's space.

When the lights come on I close my eyes to keep the pictures there a second longer. I can still see iguanas and tortoises and blue-footed boobies. I hear the narrator say, "A place to begin," and it makes a little glass-ringing sound inside my head.

Stranger things could happen. Losers win the lottery every day.

But when I open my eyes I see the back of Erik's head. Oh yeah, reality. I'll be working at the Lucky Penny this summer, signing up for dental hygiene classes in the fall. What this guy is talking about isn't the lottery. He's talking about a scholarship contest. That takes a grand to sign up for. That my gorgeous and brilliant ex-boyfriend will no doubt enter and win because he's brilliant and gorgeous, and has lots of extra space to work with now that it's not being sucked up by me.

I reach over and nudge Jonathon. "Hey," I say. "Time to wake up."

"So I'll leave some flyers here with the schedule for the prep class," says Pete the biology guy. "Everyone is welcome."

Everyone is welcome. But only Erik and I pick up flyers.

7

# Skein:

*A V formation that birds fly in
to avoid being a drag.*

All the way to pick up the boys from school, I see that stupid movie with its weird tortoises, dolphins, and birds. So many crazy birds. When the boys load up, feet and backpacks fly everywhere. I almost don't notice when Brett climbs into the seat behind me that he has a scratch on his face. Except it's a whopper.

"Did you get attacked by a cougar?"

Brett gives me the disgusted look. His favorite facial expression.

"Who did you fight with?"

"Nobody," he says.

"How come the school didn't have Mom come get you?"

"Nobody answered," says Brett. He climbs in the very back of Moby.

"That's a whole lot of nobody." I pull my homemade first-aid kit, complete with pocket knife and granola bars, out of the glove box, retrieve some antibiotic ointment, and pass it back. "What happened?"

Andrew shrugs his shoulders. Ever since Andrew got into sixth grade he acts like he's entered a universe where the rest of us don't exist. I'm not sure who Brett tells stuff to anymore, because it isn't me. But I hope Mom at least notices he looks like the Frankenstein monster.

When I get home Mom is in the laundry room pairing socks. We have a lot of socks at our house. "You're late," says Mom.

Mom cleans offices. She leaves before dinner each day and then I take over with dinner and kids. She hates working nights, but this way Danny doesn't have to go to day care and all the stuff that goes with six kids gets paid for. I'll say this for my mom, she knows how to work.

Instead of answering, I grab two black socks and fold them together.

"We heard about this stupid scholarship today, in biology."

"Why is it stupid?"

"Because you have to have money to apply. If you win, you have to pay part of the cost of going on the trip."

"How much is it?

"A thousand dollars."

"Pretty stupid," she says. "Danny has an ear infection. I need to pick up his prescription before I go to work." She grabs the keys, says hello to the boys who have their heads lodged in the cupboard, and leaves without noticing Brett's face.

Danny is sitting in the chair with his head on his arms. When he lifts his face I see that he's covered in graham cracker. He's so sleepy it's almost not disgusting. Danny is always sweetest when he's sick.

"Hi," I say. I put my hand to his forehead and it's warm.

I make a snack of butterfly oranges for all the boys. It's a thing Mom used to do for Melyssa and me when we were little. Before she had so many miscarriages, and then babies, and then had to go back to work. Maybe I just remember it this way, but I think she was a lot different back then. I flip two sides of an orange together on the plate. Not exactly filling but it looks pretty. I flap the wings at Danny on the plate, but he looks at me blankly. "How do you like it?" I say.

Danny picks up a wing and squeezes it.

Carson says, "Can we have a story about butterflies?"

The older boys look up at me, disgusted, but they don't run off. We all know they're getting too cool for this.

"Once there was a butterfly that was afraid of heights. So he walked."

Andrew says, "Butterflies can't walk."

"I don't like it," says Danny.

Brett holds up his hand with a downturned thumb.

"No butterflies then. There's going to be killing and maiming and bloodshed."

"Pirates?" says Carson.

Andrew holds his thumb up. Brett rolls his eyes. Danny is doing something with his nose that I'd rather not describe, and I take it as a wait-and-see vote.

"Pirates it is then. Our story begins in a land called Deadendia, a once happy land that was cursed by dark air that came from a nearby troll-infested mountain. The smoke was so enchanted with misery that the people never even tried to escape. They just walked around being cursed until they keeled over and died. And sometimes to cheer themselves up, they kicked each other on the street or threw rocks at innocent animals. Then one day, right in the middle of a perfectly good misery session, a pirate ship of scurvy dogs sailed to their less advantaged shores."

"The pirates were dogs?" said Danny.

"No, they were pirates. Scurvy ones," I say. "The villagers were amazed. No one ever came to Deadendia, at least not on purpose. The head pirate swung from his ship and began to tell a tale of another land with fire-breathing mountains and dragons that swam underwater and sprayed boiling water out of their noses. The people laughed at the pirate and told him he had to pay a harbor fee if he was planning on keeping his boat in town overnight. But there were a few souls that were caught up by his tale, a few crazed souls who longed to join him in spite of certain danger. . . ."

The phone rings. I pick up.

"Hi," says Melyssa. Her voice is high and breathy.

"Hi," I say. I'm lost in Deadendia.

"I . . . Zeke and I had a fight."

"How bad?" I say.

"He took his stuff."

This gets my attention. As far as I know Melyssa has never had a fight with Zeke before. They always just do what she wants.

"What did you fight about?"

She chokes up a little and then lets her words spray like a fire hydrant. "He lives on his scholarship and this measly trust fund. If we get married and have a baby it won't be enough and he'll have to work. He says he can't write and go to school and work because he'll flunk out. I work and I've got a 4.0."

"And you probably pointed that out to him, I guess."

She chokes up again. "Well, I can't help it if I'm smarter than he is."

"No, I guess not."

She blows her nose and starts crying again.

"Are you okay?" I ask.

"No."

"Do you want to come home for a while?"

"I want to come home, home."

"Home, home? But you aren't done with school." I'm talking to myself as much as to Melyssa. I'll be camping in the yard if she comes.

She says, "I can't go to school like this. I'm a mess."

"You're going to drop out? You'll lose your scholarship."

"I'm going to get a medical extension."

I'm trying to think about her, or at least sound like it. "Until when?"

"Until I feel better," she says. "Which is most likely never. I can't believe he left."

I'd like to tell her not to worry, but I can't.

The boys are staring at me when I hang up the phone.

"So who's going?" asks Andrew.

"Going where?"

"With the pirates," says Brett with disgust.

"Oh, I have to tell you tomorrow night. It's a surprise."

"Aw," says Carson.

"I hate surprises," says Andrew.

I nod my head. "You should all go play outside."

As bad as things are in Deadendia, I think they are about to get a whole lot worse.

# 8

# Molting:
*Dropping old feathers to get new ones.*

On Monday nights I leave the kids with Dad and work at the Lucky Penny. That's one of the nights Erik works too. Howard puts Erik at the front counter and me in the back, making shakes. It's not that Howard's being considerate or anything. It's just that Callie told him I might throw up in the ice cream if I had to stand next to Erik.

Making shakes is not brain surgery, but you have to keep your wits about you. For one thing, if you don't hold the cold steel cup you blend with just right, you send ice cream flying. For another thing, you have to get a feel for how the ice cream blends with what you're mixing so the shake doesn't come out runny. If the shake doesn't stand up out of the cup when I'm done, I'll pay for it myself and start over. The last thing is that you have to clean the blender blades as you go. You can't just stick the blade with grasshopper shake all over it into a pumpkin shake. You have to blend the blades in water until they're completely clean, which is time-consuming and drives Erik nuts, because patience isn't exactly his best thing.

So when the entire population of Salty Breeze Retirement Home comes in and pretty much orders enough ice cream to plug every artery they have left, and then Erik comes back with a shake in his hand and says, "They wanted Chocolate Banana Caramel, not Peanut Butter Chocolate," I'm going about eighty in a twenty-five, if you know what I mean.

"Where's the order?" I say.

Erik rolls his eyes. "I don't know. They said they didn't order this."

"Show me the order," I say. I know he has the receipt on a pin out front, and when there's a mistake that costs money we're supposed to find out whose fault it is.

"I don't have time," Erik says. "Just do it over."

A truckload of adrenaline races to my head. "Can I see the order?" I ask.

"I know you're upset," he says, laying it on thick. Like I'm one of those old women out there who just lost her teeth in a sundae.

I've covered for Erik since I started working here. He messes up about once a week because he's so good with customers he forgets to be good with typing in the right code. But I'm not covering for a patronizing me-dumper.

I put the shake I'm making down on the counter. Everyone stops what they're doing and looks at me. I walk out to the cash register and pull the receipt off the pin. I look at the order. The prehistoric woman who ordered the shake, who obviously thinks she's caught me at something, stares me down.

I walk back to Erik and show him the receipt. "You put in the code for Peanut Butter Chocolate. I'll make another one, but I'm not paying for it."

Everyone looks at Prince Charming now.

"This is just stupid," he says, and takes the receipt out of my hand. Erik looks innocent, but there is a reason he wins on the track field. And it isn't because he loves running. It's because he loves to win. He has to.

"Don't you mean *I'm* stupid?" I say.

The back room silence brings Howard charging in. He says, "Holy hell. We've got the whole town out there. You two get to work. Myra, don't be a bitch about this just because he dumped you for what's-her-boobs out there."

I look at Erik. He has what's-her-boobs guilt written all over him.

Erik says to Howard, "Myra's just been under a lot of pressure lately. You know how she gets."

What a stroke of genius to make me look like a whack job while pretending to care what kind of pressure I'm under. Who finished Erik's paper on morphology when he had a track meet all weekend? Who convinced Erik's dad it was a recycling project when his dad found beer cans in his truck?

Howard guffaws. "Yeah, I know the kind of pressure you give her, buddy. Those Morgan girls . . . they're all about pressure."

Yeah. That does it.

I take off my apron, fold it, and hand it to Callie, who's practically wetting her pants. I walk out of the Lucky Penny through the back door so I don't have to see what's-her-boobs.

The crazy part is that when I'm driving home, instead of thinking about how I've lost my job and been called a slut from a family of sluts, I think of those dirty blades of ice cream. You never think about the clean-up when you're eating those big chunks of Oreo, but you would if someone didn't do it. And that's the thing about cleaning things up—it sucks to do it and it sucks if you don't.

# 9

# Mounted Specimen:

*A stuffed bird skin that people hang on their walls because it looks pretty but doesn't make a mess.*

There are two kinds of jobs in Landon:

> (1) Rotten.
> (2) Less rotten, unless you're a dentist like Erik's dad, which actually I don't think is all that great except the money, no matter what I told Erik.

And there are two kinds of people in this town:

> (1) Losers: We work for the other kind of people.
> (2) Winners: There aren't many of these types. They move.

Of course there are variations. You can be a First Lieutenant Loser, like Howard, or an Assistant to the Winners, like my dad. He is an engineer for the copper mine. Or like my mom, who has a loser job cleaning offices until late at night, but thinks it's okay because it makes it so she can be home in the daytime with Danny. But if you are a high school senior with no skills but baby busting, food flipping, and cleaning crew, you probably shouldn't quit your job because your boss and your ex-boyfriend are jerks. That really limits where you can work around here.

So when I go home early my parents are less than thrilled. I give them the overview minus the specifics of Howard calling my sister and me sluts. When I finish, my dad, the engineer, wants to hear the story again.

"What do you mean?" he says when I get to the part where I walked to the front so I could get the receipt.

"I didn't do it."

"Erik deserves a swift kick in the butt, but you quit in the middle of a shift? What happened to everyone else when you left?"

"What happens to *you* without a job?" says Mom. "How are you going to pay for dental assistant school?"

"I don't know."

Dad says, "Maybe you should have thought of that before you let your temper get the better of you. This is exactly what that little puke wanted you to do."

*Maybe it was what I wanted me to do,* is what I want to say. But what comes out is, "I know."

Sitting at the kitchen table with bills and a checkbook stacked in front of her, Mom looks as tired as I feel. In her jagged voice she says, "We just can't do it all, Myra. Now that we have to pay for an uninsured baby there is no way we can pay for your dental hygiene class. What are you going to do without that job?"

No matter how bad I feel, my parents can always make me feel worse. "I'll start looking tomorrow after school."

"I guess you heard Melyssa is moving home?"

"Yeah, I know," I say with more frustration than I mean to.

My mom leans backward, away from her pile of bills, and sticks her pen in her gray-streaked ponytail. "Well, I guess you know everything then," she says.

Dad looks at me and Mom and sighs. I bet he wishes he could stay at work. Where everything is logical, and there are a lot less women. If only everything could be as beautiful and tidy as a smelter the height of the Empire State Building.

"I don't think you will have trouble getting another job, actually," says Dad.

I didn't see that coming.

"No, I don't," he says. "You're capable. You take care of a lot around here. I've seen you hustle around that ice-cream parlor. You're a hard worker. You work a lot harder than plenty of people I pay union wage."

I say, "Thanks, Dad." Maybe there are some things I don't know.

"But," he says, putting his finger to his nose like he does when he's measuring something, "you have to get that money for school. So you'll just have to go out there and find a new job tomorrow. Or your mom will make you pour the cement with us."

"I still need you here after school until your dad gets home," she says.

"I'll work it out," I say.

I guess this isn't the time to tell them that I want the money to go as far away from this place as I can imagine.

# 10

# Homing:
*When a bird comes home after getting lost.*

Up until Melyssa graduated a year and a half ago we shared a room, sort of. She's a night-person-talks-in-her-sleep slob and I'm a crack-of-dawn neatness freak. We survived because she was never home once she hit ninth grade. Now that she's back, pregnant and miserable with nothing to do but be high maintenance, it's likely we are going to kill each other.

It's Friday afternoon, I've had the week from Hades, and Mel's junk is everywhere.

Mel says, "So you told Old Howie to stick it, huh?"

"I didn't say anything. I just quit."

"I'll bet you folded up your apron and walked out politely."

I really hate it when she pegs me.

She says, "At least you quit, right? That's good."

"It would be good—if I had a job."

"Oh, you can get one of those. You're like a poster girl for all those waitress-nanny jobs. I mean look at you. You're like Domestic Goddess Barbie."

I sit down on the floor to put my things in stacks so I can figure out a way to put them away in half as much space. I want to very neatly die of sadness. Normally I would let Mel say whatever, but everything hurts too much right now already. "I do other things besides mop the floor and babysit."

Melyssa rolls around on her bed like a pill bug. She's not even big yet, but she acts like she weighs four hundred pounds. She sighs. "I'm not knocking it. Martha Stewart is totally smart."

"I'm not Martha Stewart."

"You iron your money and put it in order in your wallet."

Carson runs into the room. He still thinks it's like Christmas because Melyssa's home. "Mel, come see what Myra made under my bed. It has a lake made out of a milk jug and mountains out of egg cartons with little wire plants and everything."

Melyssa raises her eyebrows. "Little wire plants? Good job, Martha."

I don't answer. Thankfully they both leave so I can shove my underwear into storage baggies without being psychoanalyzed. When Melyssa comes back she says, "Maybe you could get a job making little wire plants. That's a unique skill."

I say, "Are you going to go back to school after you have the baby?"

She lies back down on the bed and pats her bulging stomach. "Don't worry. I'm not staying in this room for the rest of my life. What are *you* going to do after graduation?"

I shrug my shoulders. Right now I'm concentrating on getting through the morning.

"I heard Mom say you want to be a dental assistant."

"That was Erik's idea. But Mom and Dad are all set on it. I said I was thinking about it, but I'm not now." It's surprising to hear the words out loud.

"No?" She looks over at me. "You have something else in mind?"

"I don't know."

"You can tell Big Sis."

"Big Sis, would it be possible for you to put your socks inside your drawer?"

"Don't change the subject."

"What subject?"

"Are you going to be a topless dancer? Chimp trainer? Politician? What?"

"I don't know, really. This guy came to biology and talked about a scholarship contest where you can go on a trip that sounds . . . you know, far away."

"Science, huh. I can see that. You could kill things, sterilize them, and then organize them. That's perfect for you."

"I don't care about science. I want to get out of town. But for me to go they'd have to pick my proposal out of all the others written by the genius kids applying and I have to raise money. A lot of money."

"Where do they go?" She's sitting up now.

"It doesn't matter. I'd have to raise a thousand dollars by May."

She whistles through her teeth. "Spill it."

"The Galápagos Islands." I'm sorry the moment the words fall out of my mouth.

"No way."

"I'd have to write a research proposal that's better than Erik's."

"You'd be competing against Prince Charming?" She laughs and then she laughs again. "Now, that's perfect."

I pair my socks. Telling Melyssa is proof of my stupidity.

She says, "Wow. Do you want to do it?"

"No."

Melyssa adjusts one of my favorite pillows under her rear end. "You only go around once. And the ride ends sooner than you think."

I want to get a ride out of this room. I want to be with Erik and tell him how crazy Melyssa makes me, except I can't because I'm a dumped space-sucker. I say, "I'm not you, Mel. I can't just be brilliant on command."

Mel adjusts the pillow again and then takes it out from under her and throws it at the wall. "No. You aren't me. But you know what the real difference is?"

The list of the ways that Melyssa and I are different could fill my journal, and has pretty regularly, since I was old enough to feel inadequate. She won so many awards and trophies in high school, Dad built her a special shelf. When she left I filled it with a vase of dried flowers and a picture of me with Erik at the state fair. I stare at the mound of socks on the floor. Most of them are white but none of them matches. How can I have so many abandoned socks? How does this happen?

Mel says, "The difference is that I go after things. Even when I make a mess, at least I go after what I want."

The irony is painful. Unless Mel's big dream has always been to be pregnant, not go to school, and live in her old bedroom and not speak to her baby's father.

She says, "You should do it, Myra. You'd look great in a bikini and a headlamp. You could be Biology Barbie. Plus it would completely piss off Prince Charming."

"I'm not trying to make Erik mad. I just want to go somewhere. *Do* something."

My sister sits up slowly on the bed and crosses her legs under her. Her eyes are lit up like the old Mel, the one who cut my hair off with dull scissors when we were four and six. She says, "You can't go at this like a kindergarten teacher, Myra. If you do this, you need to win. Make him sorry for every broken promise he ever made to you. Can you do that?"

"Probably not," I say.

"Come on, Myra!" she says, her voice suddenly hard. "Don't end up like me and Mom."

I look up out of my cloud of self-pity. "What's that supposed to mean?"

She stands up and starts putting away her stuff.

I wait. "Mel?"

"What?" she says.

I wait. Mel can't stand silence.

She keeps her hunched back to me. She says, "I thought you knew."

"I'm not going to guess about this."

"Haven't you ever wondered about my birthday?"

I stand up alongside Mel. I am six inches taller than she is now. It's like talking to one of the boys. I say, "I don't spend a lot of time thinking about your birthday."

She puts her hands in her pockets. "I mean, have you ever wondered about that story Mom and Dad tell about how I was premature?"

I say, "Why would I wonder about that? Mom miscarries if you look at her wrong."

"Because I wasn't seven weeks early."

It takes a second for this to sink in. Then I say, "You're kidding, right?" Mel doesn't laugh. I sit back down on the floor in between all my unmatched socks. Mel sits down next to me.

Mel lowers her voice and puts her head close to mine. "Mom told me when I was fourteen. She wanted to scare me. I thought she'd tell you too."

"Mom was pregnant when they got married? Are you sure?"

"I don't think she'd lie about it," she says.

I pick up a sock in my hand and squeeze it. Moms aren't supposed to start off their families by getting knocked up. At least not my mom. She gets mad if I wear my swimming suit to the city pool without a tank top. And what about my dad?

The engineer who never does anything illogical, immoral, or embarrassing?

There is too much in my head to fit it all.

"I'm not like her," says Mel. "I'm not going to marry Zeke and have a bunch of kids just because of this. No way. That's what I'm saying. You don't have to take the hand you get, just because you got it. Going on this trip . . ."

I stand back up. I have to get out of this house. Everything is dirty in this house. "Who cares about this trip? You just told me Mom was knocked up when she got married."

"Lower your voice, hysterics girl. It's not like it doesn't happen. I'm just saying you have to make your own rules, you know. You don't have to settle."

I walk out of the room. I stand in the hallway that is barricaded by my brothers' toys. There are messes everywhere. I can't get out and there is nowhere to go. I walk back in and get a laundry basket. I start throwing my clothes in the basket as fast as I can.

"You can't tell Mom I told you."

I grab a stack of shirts and fling them into my basket. "Just stop talking. I'm moving to the basement."

My mother walks into the room. "What's going on? Why do you two have to yell?"

I look at my mother and I feel so incredibly lied to. She had to marry Dad. He had to marry her. No wonder he married her. And then they kept having us. If she hadn't miscarried so often there might be a school bus of us.

Mel says, "Myra's moving to the basement."

Mom shakes her head. "I'm sorry you can't keep the room to yourself, Myra. I am. I know you like things clean. But what else are we going to do?"

"Don't worry about it," I say. "I'm moving downstairs."

"Don't be ridiculous."

My mother glares at both of us. As if we're five and seven again. Same old story: Melyssa starts the fire and I take the heat. My mom's tired eyes rest on me. "It's not a perfect world for any of us."

"No kidding," I say.

I grab my jeans and throw them on my growing pile. The basement is unfinished so it's filthy and about two degrees warmer than sleeping outside. It's filled with stacks of things we don't know what to do with. The windows are small and the light is dim. It has spiders. But it will be quiet. It will be away from Melyssa and my mom.

BBD (before being dumped) I could escape from here with Erik. Now there is nowhere to go but down.

I step over my brother's toys and walk to the basement door. I kick it open with my foot and begin my descent.

# 11

# Pecking Order:
*Who's in charge.*

At five I look over at my alarm clock vibrating on the cement floor. I've survived my first night in the dungeon. I get out of my sleeping bag and grab my pen flashlight so I can find the light switch without killing myself on the junk spread all over the floor. The fact that I could go to sleep in this subzero pig pen is a sure sign I'm in denial.

I go upstairs to shower and thaw. I write a note to my parents telling them that I'm going to a prep class for the AP biology test, which I feel guilty about, but it's not totally a lie so I do it anyway. They're going to be mad about me taking Moby, but I'll be back before anybody's even out of their pajamas.

Right before I walk out the door Carson wanders into the dark kitchen. "Where are you going?"

"I have a class."

He rubs his eyes and looks me over. "It's Saturday."

"It's a special class."

"Who's going to make me breakfast?"

I go to the cupboard and quietly get his favorite cereal and a bowl. "All you have to do is get the milk. But go back to bed first. It's too early."

"What time will you be back?" he says.

"Right after breakfast."

He walks down the shadowy hallway. I wait until I hear him get in his bed. I count to ten to make sure he keeps the light off, and then I leave.

I turn on Moby. The Suburban makes a racket in the cold. I watch for the lights to go on in my parents' room but they don't. Not even a flicker. I put my head on the steering wheel for a second, trying to get the guts to drive away.

I can't believe my mom was pregnant before they got married. How could they have done that? How could they have not told me all these years? Is that why Mel got pregnant? Do I come from a habitually reproducing family? Am I next?

I *was* almost next.

I bob my head on the steering wheel. This is stupid. I can't raise money or write a science paper that's better than Erik's. But when I go to turn off the car, I look back at the dark windows of my house. I know I will suffocate if I go back inside.

I drive to the Great Salt Lake State Marina on the winding road that leads past the edges of the plant, with gray trucks and gray tailings piles and gray fences and a gigantic smelter. The weather has turned cold again, but there is no snow or rain to soften the edges of the wind. I drive through the park gate and pull in next to the office. I see Erik's white truck. Of course he would be early.

When I walk into the room I'm surprised by the number of kids who are desperate enough for a vacation to be here this morning. There must be almost a dozen of us. But then most of these kids actually care about school. They're the average-raisers that I parted ways with in junior high. They probably get up at this time of day every Saturday.

The room we're meeting in also surprises me. I follow the other kids past the front desk into a clubhouse-looking room with couches and tables. There are trophies lining the bookshelves and tiny flags plastered on the walls. It's more like someone's living room than a classroom.

When I walk in I see Erik talking to some pasty-faced goth girl. He sees me and his eyebrows shoot up, but he doesn't say anything. I force myself to keep walking to a chair. *I can do this,* I promise myself. If I'm going to get out of this town, away from moments of torture just like this, I'm going to have to live through this morning.

At the front of the room is Pete the biology guy. He's wearing the same clothes he was when he came to our class. He waits until everyone is seated and then says, "Welcome to the Galápagos project training class. If you're here for home ec you're in the wrong room."

Everyone laughs, even Erik. It's a little less funny to me.

"Seriously, we're having the meeting here because I thought it would be nicer to be near the subject that you will be writing about."

A tall black kid with a buzz says, "I thought we were writing about the Galápagos Islands, not Utah's toilet water."

"That toilet water is the closest thing in Utah to the Galápagos Islands and a wonderful place to learn about scientific writing," says Pete. "How about we go around and introduce ourselves, starting with the comedian in the front row. "

"Pritchett," says the kid with the buzz. He puts his hands out and nods at everyone, like the applause light just went off over his head. "And I'll be here all week."

There should be a rule against people trying to be funny before the sun comes up.

After all the introductions detailing how mutantly intelligent everyone but me is, Pete gets down to basics. "Today we're going to talk about environment. Who can describe the environment of the Galápagos?"

"They're islands on the equator," says the goth girl. She introduced herself as Dawn. I think I might call her Dusk myself.

"It's a series of islands primarily made of molten rock and is shaped by the confluence of the ocean currents Humboldt, Panama, and Cromwell," says Pritchett.

"Funny and smart," says Pete.

An ROTC type named Alex twists his pen in his hand. Next to him are not one but two Megans, and a kid who looks like his glasses weigh more than he does.

Erik raises his hand. "It's an archipelago of volcanic islands distributed around the equator in the Pacific Ocean 972 kilometers west of continental Ecuador."

"Someone else has done their homework. Erik, is it?"

"There are fifteen large islands and three small ones with rare species found only on the islands themselves," says a kid named Ho-Bong. He and his twin brother, Ho-Jun, introduced themselves as being "transferred."

I feel nauseated. Someone should do a research paper on know-it-all preening rituals. I look out the window. The wind is making the water spit onto the glass. Two suicidal seagulls are diving through the wind currents.

Pete gives us a little pep talk about the proposal, and then passes out an assignment sheet outlining the requirements. "You are going to write a proposal for the study of flora or fauna on the Galápagos Islands, but you should look at the whole world as a research project. There are enough things to study right outside of this building to fill this room with research findings."

Pete turns to my corner of the room. "Myra, what do you find so interesting outside this building?"

I stare at him. He stares back.

He says, "Isn't there anything you like to study, just for fun?"

*What did I ever do to him?*

"You know, something you love to do so much you can't help but get all geeky about it, like baseball scores or music lyrics or something."

My mind fills with white space. Everyone looks at me. I look out the window. "Birds," I say. "I like birds."

"Nice," says Pete. "Any special kind?"

"Seagulls and stuff." I could die at how stupid I sound.

"I'm a gull geek myself. Which one is your favorite?"

"I don't know. The Utah one."

Pete says, "You mean *Larus californicus*, the California gull?"

The know-it-all Pritchett snickers.

Pete doesn't miss a beat. "Actually Myra brings up an interesting point. The majority of Utahans identify this bird as a 'sea' gull, even in published texts, when in fact science has named this gull for its land origins, and it's a state bird that is named after another state. Great, Myra. So, something around here that you can observe and learn about that we might otherwise take for granted."

The amazing thing is that even though I know that Pete is just trying to smooth over how stupid I am, the fact that he is being nice about it makes me relax. I look over at Erik. He's smirking. I'd never smirk at him. Even now.

Erik says, "Are you going to pick the winners for the scholarship, Pete?"

"No," says Pete, laughing. "And hell no."

The two Megans look at each other. Alex stops spinning his pen.

We're from Utah. Teachers don't swear in class, unless a bookshelf falls on their foot or the world ends.

Pete says, "Important people with suits pick the winner. I don't even get to go myself. I'm here to help you get excited about the project, like a science cheerleader."

"You cheer?" says Pritchett.

Pete nods seriously. "I've got moves."

"Let's see one," says Dawn. I'm going to guess and say she doesn't like cheerleaders.

Pete looks over the room. Then he climbs up on his chair. He puts his butt in the air and purses his lips. I can't believe this. His neck starts bobbing around. He snaps his fingers and sways:

> "You might be good at basketball
>
> You might be good at track
>
> But when it comes to the Galápagos
>
> You might as well step back,
>
> Might as well step back!
>
> Say what?
>
> You might as well step back!
>
> Can't hear you!
>
> Show me those blue-footed boobies!
>
> Go Galápagos!"

Pritchett says, "You are so white."

"Can't be helped," says Pete.

No one else says anything. You can tell everyone thinks Pete's insane. Because he is. He bows and jumps off his chair. When he hits the ground he's the mild-mannered graduate student again.

"Well, that does it for today. If you have questions, here's my e-mail and cell." He writes his info on the board. Teachers never give out their numbers in school. They don't even tell us their first names.

A few students stay behind to ask questions and suck up to Pete, including Erik. I have a question, but I want to get out of there so I don't have to watch Erik ignore me. I already feel like chewed gum. I walk outside. I remind myself that Erik's just another person now. Except he's not. He's Erik, beloved by adults, kids, and even haters like Jonathon. So all I can think is that if I was a better person he would still want me. But he doesn't.

And now he's the competition.

I stand in the walkway to the building, wondering if I should go back in and ask Pete my question about my topic, or namely my lack of a topic. But I can't because Erik's in there.

I busy myself looking at the posting board on the front of the building. It's pretty all-purpose. Pictures of boats for sale. Information about cleaning your boats and a description of what the weather flags mean. Down at the bottom of the board there is also one "Help Wanted" sign. I reread it. They are looking for a secretary at the marina.

I write down the number. That would be perfect—except that I'm in school. I write it down anyway.

"You thinking about getting a job here?" says Erik. His voice makes me jump.

I turn around. "Maybe."

"Don't get mad. Just asking."

"I'm not mad." I know my face is flushed. "There aren't a lot of jobs around town."

"I'm sorry this has been so hard on you," he says.

"What's been hard on me?"

"Come on. I can see you're upset."

"I'm fine," I say. *Of course he can see I'm upset, because the world stops without him, right?*

"So you really want to go to the Galápagos Islands?"

"Why wouldn't I?"

He smiles that perfectly straightened and bleached smile of his. "It just doesn't seem like your thing."

"Why wouldn't it be *my thing*?"

He tips his head. "You always get so defensive. I just mean that I don't think you would like to travel that far."

"People can surprise you," I say.

"I hope you get the job then," says Erik, his voice lifting and then sticking straight in my chest. With a single stroke, whether I get the job or not, I'm a loser.

Pete walks out of the room with the twins in front of him. Pete locks the door behind him.

"You all right?" he says to me.

"Sure," I say, steadying my voice.

"Good. Well, hey, do you really like gulls?"

The two guys with Pete scan me with their superconductor brains and then give me the "nice try" look.

"Yeah," I say. "I mean, I haven't studied them in books, but I like watching them."

"Great. We're all going to go out next week to do a little observation. You have a topic yet?"

"Actually I have a question about that."

Pete nods to team Ho. "See you next week, guys."

They walk away from us, still giving me disgusted looks.

"Fire away."

"Well, what if I don't have the money by May first?"

"It's a lot of money, isn't it?"

"Yeah," I say. "If I had an extra month . . ."

"No can do. The donor said he wouldn't fudge on the amount or the deadline. Has this thing about being self-sufficient, building character, and all that horse hockey."

"Guess I better build some character fast then."

"That shouldn't be too hard for you." He smiles and I feel funny. Not ha-ha funny. But wow-you-have-nice-eyes-for-a-teacher funny.

*He's my teacher,* I think. *Get a grip!*

He says, "See you next week, Myra."

*He's not actually my teacher. He's just helping us do our proposals. No. Bad. Bad Myra.*

He walks to the parking lot and gets into a prehistoric Volkswagen van, the kind you see in old movies where everyone is a tragic hippie. It doesn't look like it should be allowed on the highway. For starters, it doesn't have a back passenger window. After Pete fiddles around in his van he drives back over to me. He's wearing fingerless gloves, a beanie, and a puffy coat. "Here's a book on flightless cormorants. I had it in the back of my van. You might like them for a topic."

I look down at the book and see a brown bird with exotic turquoise eyes. I read the title, *Galápagos Cormorants: The Jewels of Isabela.*

"Thanks," I say.

"I think these birds might suit you."

"Okay." I wonder how he knows what will suit me.

"And there's a glossary of terms in there to teach you the lingo. You'll be thinking like an ornithologist in no time." He waves his fingerless-gloved hand at me and rattles away into the gray air.

There ought to be a rule about people being so cool you can't stand it. But I don't think rules are Pete's thing.

# 12

# Echolocation:
*Finding your way in the dark.*

When I walk through the door to my house, the phone is ringing. No one is answering. I rush to the phone. Involuntary Erik expectations.

"Is this Myra?" says a loud, raunchy voice. Not only is it not Erik, it's Howard, my delightful ex-boss.

"Yes," I say, with about as much interest as I have in eating dirt.

"Do you want to work here or not?"

"Hi, Howard."

Mom, who is standing nearby, perks up.

"Are you thinking you're going to get a raise out of this?"

"No," I say. "I wasn't thinking that."

"Well, how about fifty more cents an hour? That'll buy you some nail polish."

I can do a lot of things, like clean a toilet, go without lunch, and sleep in a disgusting basement. But I cannot go back to the Lucky Penny. "Thanks, Howard. But I don't think that's a good idea." I know I'm saying no to a job and a raise. But if I go back I'm lost.

Howard's voice is loud. "Hell, I'll fire him if it makes you feel better. He's a pain in the butt anyway."

If he fires Erik for me, no one will wonder who messed up on that order. And Erik will have to look for a job. But I'd still be working for a guy who makes "those Morgan girls" jokes.

I say, "No. It's probably for the best."

"Better think about this, honey. Jobs aren't growing on trees around here. I could make you a day manager as soon as school gets out."

"No, thanks," I say.

His voice jabs through the phone. "Suit yourself. But don't count on me for a reference!" He slams down the phone.

*He* won't give ME a reference. I could write a reference for him, but they wouldn't put an ad for that job in the paper. Before I even hang up Mom is marching, still in her pajamas, off into the front yard. I follow her. Dad is pulling out of the driveway. She gets up to his window and says, "Howard called to give her the job back and she turned him down."

Dad looks at me. I know he doesn't care if I keep working at that hole, but he has to side with Mom. Those are the rules of peace in my house. He says, "You can't be too picky, Myra."

"Is there anything I can do at the plant?" I say.

"Let's talk when you aren't in school."

"But I need to make money now." The whine in my voice surprises me.

"Why?" says Mom, looking curious.

"I need to get some money saved away for school and stuff. It's coming up quick."

Dad says, "You'll figure it out. Life's a do-it-yourself project." Then he pulls away.

"If you want to be a hardhead you have to expect a few hard knocks," says Mom.

Is there a manual somewhere that teaches parents these expressions? I walk my hard head past her into the house. I need something to clean. I head for the dungeon.

The thing about the basement is that it's uncleanable. That's why Mom would rather pour patio cement than try to fix it up. Down here, you can shove things to the side or sweep a square foot here and there, but there isn't anywhere to put things away. And no adult in this house seems capable of throwing out the old furniture, boxes of papers and books, old clothes, old toys, stale food storage, and plain old junk.

I stand at the bottom of the stairs, armed with a lamp I have rescued from the furniture discard pile. I plug it in and start imagining the basement divided into tidy, organized sections. After a minute or two my brain cramps. Sometimes you just have to admit defeat before you start.

I sit on my sleeping bag and go through my backpack for things I've gathered up. More than a clean living space I need a job. Fast.

"Can I camp with you?" says Carson from the top of the stairs. His voice startles me.

"It's not camping unless you're outside," I say.

He plods down the steps. "Why are you sleeping in the basement then?"

"I'm in exile," I say.

"I'll exile with you. It's cool."

"Freezing is more like it," I say. "Now I have to do some work."

Carson runs back up the stairs, but then parks himself on the top step.

I say, "I'll help you with your dinosaur trees tonight if you stop watching me."

"Danny stepped on my lagoon."

"And I'll fix the lagoon."

"Deal," he says, and disappears.

I sharpen a few pencils. I make a list:

**My Job Experience:**
Ice Cream Server. No References.

**My Job Requirements:**
Must be part-time
Must require no experience
Must pay enough to raise money for the contest
Must not be totally disgusting and humiliating

First I call the marina and get an answering machine, which doesn't surprise me. It's not like people are sailing a lot in February. Then again, the sign I saw was a recent posting, and the machine says I can leave a message, so I do.

Next, I scratch out the last part of my requirements with one of my extrasharp pencils. I can live with humiliating, maybe even disgusting, if it will get me the money I need to apply. The biology guy said the secret to survival is adaptation. I go through the local want ads, crossing out the jobs that require me to work during school, operate heavy machinery, or commute to Egypt and back. I'm left with five jobs.

I take a break and skim the book that Pete gave me. There are forty kinds of cormorants, or shags, and they are pretty common. We have double-crested cormorants on the Great Salt Lake. But the kind in the Galápagos is flightless and totally bizarre. They have little tiny wings that only work as rudders underwater. Scientists think that they didn't have any use for flying because it was too far to go back to the mainland, so they just gave up and became swimmers.

Then suddenly it drives me wild that Pete thinks this bird is a good topic for me. What does he mean when he says these birds "might suit me"? Am I flightless? Forever grounded? Marooned in Landon?

I put Pete's dumb book away and pull out my list of job possibilities. Flightless. I'll show him flightless.

At the top of my list is a job in a clothing store. I make a phone call. "Hi, I'm calling about the stock girl—"

"Filled it." *Click.*

I call the next two numbers and get the same basic response, although the other people let me finish my sentence. I have to give myself a Galápagos cheer to get the nerve to make the next call. *You might as well step back. Go Galápagos!* I'm not sure I can handle it if I get this job.

"Chicken Little."

I say, "I'm calling about the ad you have for a personal advertiser."

"You have to dress up in chicken suit." My worst germ fears are realized.

"Has the job been taken?"

"If you want an interview you better come meet me."

"I'll be right in."

"Suit yourself," says the crusty voice on the other end of the line.

I announce to my cheerless mother that I have an interview. She's out back pounding a frame board for the patio and I make her miss. "For what?" she says, shaking her hand.

"Public relations," I say, and whip back into the house before I have to explain.

Stella Handy, the owner of Chicken Little, has creases in her face older than I am. She is wearing an aqua-colored T-shirt that has LAS VEGAS written on it in cursive with sequins. We sit in folding chairs in her closet-size office at the back of the restaurant. The room smells of grease and rose perfume. I think she's giving me the evil eye, but I'm not sure. Maybe she always squints. She says, "Are you a drug user?"

"No."

"Illegal alien?"

I'm 5 foot 7, have light brown hair, pasty white skin, pale blue eyes, and freckles. I look about as foreign as a supersize cheeseburger. "Um, I was born here, if that's what you mean."

"Do you faint easy?"

This is not a question I want to be asked in a job interview. "Not really. Why?"

"Some people find the suit a little stuffy." Her lips turn down slightly. "What's your greatest asset?"

I consider this a moment. "I like things clean."

One penciled-on eyebrow rises. "You know you're applying to be a giant chicken, right?"

I smile as brightly as I can. "A chicken should be clean, don't you think?"

She doesn't smile back. "How clean are you?"

"I scrub the grout in my shower with a toothbrush."

She gathers some mucus in the back of her throat and makes a clearing sound. She rolls her neck around until it pops. I'm already thinking of where I'm going to apply next when she says, "Can you start this afternoon?"

"Are you serious?"

The crags in her face momentarily recede into a smile. "You can start wavin' your tail feathers as soon as you can get the suit on."

She opens a cabinet behind her and extracts the chicken suit. It was probably nice when she bought it a century ago. The giant yellow feathers droop with grunge. The sight of it makes me quiver.

"Is there any way to disinfect it?" I ask.

She shakes her head and narrows her gaze. "Might ruffle the feathers."

I tell myself that when I stand on the lava shores of the Galápagos Islands, I will be glad I subjected my pride and my immune system to this deep-fried torture. I take the suit and head for the bathroom. None of the inmates behind the counter looks at me. It's lunch rush. Time to sell some chicken.

Before I get dressed I make a quick phone call from my cheap-ola cell phone to my house and get Carson. Surprisingly my phone works. This phone isn't designed to do much more than call the person next door. I say, "Listen, buddy, can you tell Mom I got a job so I won't be home for a while?"

"How long until you're home?" says Carson.

"What's wrong?"

"Danny fell off his bike."

"Is he okay?"

Melyssa comes on the phone. "Hello." She sounds irritated. "Where are you?"

"Is Danny hurt?"

"He's fine."

"What happened?"

"He hit his head. Mom freaked 'cause he wasn't wearing his helmet. But he's fine."

My chest gets tight. "He has to wear a helmet. He crashes."

"Wow. Is there an echo in here? Everyone acts like I've never taken care of a kid before. Did you get a job?"

"I'm starting right now."

"Aren't you a go-getter? Where at?"

It's no use. Let the mocking begin. "The Chicken Little Drive-Thru."

"Sweet Mother of Grease."

I stare at the suit, hanging before me in all its foul splendor. I may have to tell my family I work here, but I don't have to tell them what I do. "It's a job."

"You have no shame," says Mel.

Mel's ashamed of me. The irony of my life is unending.

I hang up and reach for the suit. When I unzip it and look inside a spider climbs out. I stand paralyzed for a minute. Not by the spider, but by the idea that I'm about to put something on my body, and over my head, that has been a spider's home. Maybe there are even eggs in the suit. In all likelihood there are fleas or lice or skin-eating viruses in the flaps and folds of this death bag.

It comes down to this: How bad do I want out of this town?

Bad enough. I put on the suit.

# 13

Epigamic Display:
*When a bird dresses up and shakes its feathers
to get another bird's attention.*

I tie my head on and grab my sign. I walk past my busy co-workers and the few people who have come to eat inside. Luckily I don't recognize anyone from school. I nod my beak in greeting. Except that it's filthy, the suit is comforting, like having a big, sweaty secret identity. Instead of Wonder Woman, I'm Chicken Little. *Galápagos,* I silently chant to myself, *Galápagos.*

When I get out onto the street, the wind gusts through my beak and into the opening at my neck. I just have to humiliate myself by dancing around, jiggling a sign that says BEST-LOOKING CHICKS IN TOWN. I look through my peephole at the cars passing. People honk at me. I wave. The cold feels good. No one knows who I am. I'm getting paid.

I realize pretty quickly that I'm going to have to think of ways to entertain myself and keep my feet moving if I'm going to do this for hours. To get my mind off the spider eggs, I try to remember a few routines I did for my brothers when they were all little. I start slow, with a soft shoe that I made up for Andrew. I have to change it up a bit—a claw to the left and a claw to the right. A few more cars honk. I sway a little bigger, kicking my legs up just enough to look like I'm dancing. After a few more honks, a car with guys my age passes. One brown head hangs out the window and yells, "Nice breasts!"

The funny thing is that instead of shrinking into my three-toed boots, I'm fine. I even give a little wing in response. Inside the costume I can be as weird as I want. A few more cars go by, and then one pulls into the drive-in and parks. As they get out of the car, the middle-age couple gives me a thumbs-up. I feel so proud. I've recruited eaters! For the worst job in the world, this one isn't half bad. Okay, maybe it's half bad. But the other half is almost fun.

Around dusk I see a white truck pass out of the corner of my eye. I whirl around. It's not Erik. Maybe it is. I swear everyone in this town drives a white truck. There is too much traffic to see the head of the driver. The passenger is definitely a red-head. I tilt my beak so I can see better, but it's too late. The truck is gone.

I stand there on the street corner in my bird costume feeling ridiculous. I don't know if I can finish my shift. I want to sit down. I want to go to sleep.

It's not that Erik could have recognized me, if that was Erik. It's because someday soon Erik will be a stranger to me. I won't know anything about him except gossip. This person

I planned my life around will plan his life around some other girl—someone who isn't a space-sucker or a giant chicken.

The street is quiet for a few minutes. A dusty wind filters in through the costume. No more soft shoeing. I'm me again, in a gross suit. I stand stiffly holding the sign. Nobody honks. I should quit.

But I need the job. . . . I need the money. . . . Why should I let Erik keep me from making money? From writing a proposal for the contest? I start waving the sign a little. So what if I'm a loser. I'm not going to get fired today. *Galápagos,* I chant to myself. *Galápagos.*

As I'm waving the sign I remember how I used to love dancing when I was little. I did it to entertain my brothers but also because I loved doing it. Just because I've turned into this pathetic flightless cormorant doesn't mean I have to stay one. I can evolve. Adapt. Change. Today I can be a great flightless chicken instead. Not a huge improvement. But chickens travel.

Across the street I see the flickering of light. The traffic light glazes the asphalt in red, yellow, and green. A silhouette in a sweatshirt stands at the crosswalk, looks over at me, and leans up against the light. I turn my back and keep dancing.

I think of a video I saw on YouTube once with Mick Jagger and Tina Turner. I'm Tina, hoochie coochie-ing on those amazing legs. Then I'm Mick for a while, flapping my wings. Cars pass and honk. In my head I hear "Brown Sugar" playing. Not the dance of a space-sucker. Not the dance of Erik's invisible girlfriend. Not the dance of a bird resigned to her fate. I don't have to take millions of years to evolve. I can do it in the blink of a headlight.

Right in the middle of my crazed chicken routine, two cars race past, running the red at the intersection. They are honking at each other, windows down in spite of the cold. Luckily no one is coming so they don't kill anyone. Kids race all the time around here. There isn't all that much to do on a February night after the basketball game is over and the movies have all started. I keep dancing and flipping my sign.

Just as they pass me I hear brakes. One of the cars stops and a guy gets out. Then he runs. At me. Into me. I fly backward. My head hits the ground, but it bounces instead of splitting open because of the costume.

I go numb. Everything spins. Except the weight on top of me.

I can't see him very well—just a patch of blond hair tied in a red bandanna. A jean jacket. He jumps up and laughs. It's a forced laugh. He doesn't think this is funny either. He's just a wannabe banger trying to be cool for his loser friends. Then he's gone. And I'm flat on my back seeing stars through my peepholes. Millions of lightless stars.

Stella shows up in my peepholes a few seconds later. There are other people too.

They take off my head.

"Myra!"

In the midst of the mob of chicken workers staring at me, there is a face that shouldn't be there. I see Jonathon Hempilmeyer's nose ring. He's wearing a white sweatshirt.

He was the kid on the street corner watching me. "Myra," he says, coming close. He's holding his camera, filming me on the ground.

"Jonathon?"

Jonathon shuts off his camera and stares at me with that wide-eyed stoner look he gets. "I'm sorry. It all happened so fast. I didn't know it was you."

Everything is still spinning. But the last few minutes are all coming back to me and I'm not dead. I look at his camera. "Don't you dare post that."

Jonathon sputters. "Yeah. No. I won't."

Stella ignores Jonathon and helps me stand up. She says, "You aren't hurt. You're fine. Just walk it off. Do you want some ice cream?"

I go back into the restaurant and sit in a booth. Jonathon doesn't come in, and I'm glad because I'm almost coherent enough to tell him what a jerk he is for standing there and filming me getting knocked down. Even if he didn't know it was me. I put my chicken head on the table. I'm done evolving for the day. I drink ice water from a paper cup. One of the workers asks Stella if he should call the police.

"Of course not. She's not bleeding, is she?" She looks at me again. "You aren't bleeding, are you?"

"I'm fine," I say.

"Of course you are," says Stella.

I'm going to be fine. I just need to go home. Right after I quit this job, kill Jonathon, and go back to my pathetic, flightless life.

# 14

# Keel:

*The bone that holds muscles together
at the front of a bird so it can fly.
Flightless cormorants have a stunted keel.*

"So are you going to stay in bed all day?" says Dad.

I look at him through the slanted light of the basement windows.

"I don't feel so good," I say.

"This sulking has to stop, Myra. It's starting to upset the whole family."

"Sorry, I'm just tired," I say. I stay under my sleeping bag because I don't know if I have bruises from last night. I don't think I talked to anyone. All I remember is that I somehow made it home, put the greasy money Stella paid me in my pencil-box bank, and fell asleep in my clothes. I'm still in a semiconscious state this morning, but I know enough not to tell my dad I was tackled by a wannabe gang member.

"I know you've had some bad breaks," he says.

"Yep," I say, hoping he's not literally right.

"But we have to move on. Roll with the punches."

"I'm trying," I say. "Really."

"Did you get a job?"

"It wasn't a good job," I say.

"Honest work is good work, Myra."

I wish he wouldn't use that word. Honesty isn't this family's strong suit. But there does seem to be plenty of rolling with the punches.

"We're going for a drive. Melyssa's even going to come. . . . She had another fight with Zeke last night, and we need to get her out today."

My dad is a big fan of Sunday drives. Everyone else in our neighborhood goes to church, so I think he feels like we need our own ritual. We drive out of town. Which is a pretty good ritual if you ask me. But lately the boys fight the whole time, and if they're quiet I can hear my parents not talking. So it makes it hard to care about the scenery.

"So what about it?" he says.

"I think I'll sleep a little more," I say. I would go if I could stand up without giving the whole battered chicken thing away. And I really do have to study.

"The boys will be disappointed," he says roughly. "We were all looking forward to doing something together as a family today." He marches up the stairs with heavy feet.

That engineer dad of mine. He knows right where to dig.

By the time they get home from the drive, I've made spaghetti with meatballs and fixed Carson's dinosaur lagoon. I've also swallowed enough ibuprofen to burn a hole in my stomach. And I've scoured the Internet and seen no sign of Jonathon making my shame viral. At least I won't have to live that down on Monday.

No one talks much at dinner except to tell me that the trip was a big downer because Melyssa threw up three times, once in the car. Melyssa stays in her room while we eat.

After dinner it's late, and the boys and I lie around on the floor in the family room. Mel is out on the porch with Zeke, so we try to be quiet. Not that we want Mel and Zeke to get back together necessarily. But if they wanted to, it would be okay.

Andrew tells me in detail about all the shows he watched on TV yesterday, like a rerun without pictures. Brett doesn't talk. I'm still sore from being tackled, but I'm starting to feel better. Except for the Mel and Zeke show on the porch, it almost feels like a normal Sunday night.

When Andrew finally finishes his monologue, I talk to Brett. "So what happened to you that day, with the scratch?"

I scoot closer to him and he scoots away. Maybe if I fessed up about the bruises all over my body he'd talk too. Instead I say, "Who wants to hear what the white witch asked?"

Everyone, including Brett, moves closer.

In my best white witch voice I say, "Do you come from the land that holds the magic jewel of Isabela?"

Danny's eyes are wide.

"The pirate king called, 'Why yes, I do. Why do you ask?'"

"The white witch leaned upon her school-issue yardstick and said, 'The magic jewel that is hidden in the deadly cave of the cormorants, the precious jewel that kills trolls?'

"'So you've heard of it then,' said the pirate king.

"The crowd hushed. This was their chance to be rid of the evil stinking trolls. A magic jewel that could solve all their problems. What could be simpler? Except who could they trust to sail across the treacherous ocean to retrieve it?

"From the ranks of the miserable town stepped a band of volunteers as motley as the crew on board. Among them were scholars, noblemen, the town prince, a few maids in waiting, and a scullery maid who made a mean spaghetti sauce. But alas the pirate king had room for only two travelers. 'We must have a contest.'"

"The prince wins," says Carson. He moves in closer so he's nearly on my feet.

"You think?" I say.

"Me too," says Danny, crushing closer too. "The prince should win."

Even my brothers know I don't stand a chance. "Well, what if the prince is under a spell? Like a stupidity spell," I say.

"From the witch?" says Andrew.

"From the king and queen, who want to keep him safe from all scullery maids."

"You said it was going to be about pirates," says Brett, pinching Carson to get him out of the way.

"Stop it!" yells Carson. "I'm listening."

Mel shows up at the edge of the room. Zeke's silhouette is gone. She's crying. "Could you all just shut up? Especially you, Carson. Just shut up."

Carson's face collapses, and he runs out of the room.

"Nice, Mel," I say.

"You shut up too, Myra." She doesn't even look at me as she says this.

Mom walks in, takes one look at Mel's tears, and crosses the room to her. "Did you and Zeke fight again?"

"He's such a thoughtless jerk."

Meanwhile Carson is running down the hallway banging on things as he goes, thanks to Mel's cheer and kindness.

Mom puts her arm around Melyssa and walks her into the bedroom. The other boys and I lie quietly on the floor until they're gone.

"Melyssa's mean," says Danny.

"I can't stand her," says Andrew. "I can't wait till she moves."

I whisper, "Hey, you don't mean it."

Brett looks off into space.

I say, "Let's get some sleep."

"It's not even nine o'clock," says Andrew.

"You could go watch TV with Dad in the kitchen."

"Sweet," says Andrew, and bolts for the next room.

I hear the little TV in the next room. Whatever they are watching involves a lot of noisy gunfire. Danny crawls onto my lap. I say, "And you are going to help me cheer up Carson?"

Brett kicks at the couch. "I wish she'd move too. And I do mean it. I wish she'd take her big fat stomach and big fat mouth and get out of here."

I reach my hand out for his arm but he moves farther away.

"This isn't like one of your stupid stories," he says.

In the kitchen I hear the sound of explosions.

I say, "How do you know? You haven't heard the end of my story."

# 15

# Buffeting:
*When the weather knocks birds senseless.*

Ms. Miller offers to lend a movie on the Galápagos Islands to anyone who is interested. After class Erik sprints up to her desk. I'm still stiff from being a Chicken Sandwich, so I'm a little slower to suck up.

"I'd like to watch it too," I say, pointing to the DVD.

"Are you applying?" says Ms. Miller. She doesn't even try to hide how surprised she is.

I say, "Yes, I am."

"How nice," she says. We both look down.

"Anyone can apply, right?"

"Well, sure," she says.

That's the thing about doormats: sometimes they can slip right out from underneath you.

Erik says, "She can have it first." He smiles at Ms. Miller, like he's some sort of Boy Scout. Which of course, he is.

Ms. Miller says, "How nice of you, Erik! Don't you need to

get a start on your topic, though? Maybe you two could watch it together?"

"No," we say simultaneously.

"Oh," says Ms. Miller. She obviously has me confused with someone Erik would be seen with. "Well, then watch it tonight if you can, Myra. Erik needs to—I mean, you both need to get started as soon as possible."

"Sounds great, Ms. Miller," says Erik, in a deeply likable tenor. I wonder if anyone in the world knows the other side of Erik. Sometimes I think I've imagined it myself.

Erik says, "Myra, you should have it first." Erik starts to hand me the DVD.

I say, "I don't need to see the movie to start working. I've already picked a topic." The words pop out of my mouth before I can swallow them.

"You have?" says Erik. "That's great."

"Well, good for you, Myra," says Ms. Miller. She looks at me like she's never seen me before. "What are you going to research?"

"The flightless cormorant," I say. I am *so not* writing about that stupid bird, but I need to get out of this conversation without sounding like a complete moron, which of course I am. "They're so rare and surprising."

"Surprising is right," says Ms. Miller. She puts her hands in her lab coat pockets. I might be imagining it, but she seems like she's holding in a laugh. "Good luck to both of you. And may the best scientist win. I've been told they would prefer not to give both awards to one school, but I suppose it's possible. If you are both so much better than everyone else maybe they'd reconsider."

"That would be *great*," says Erik.

Great. Great. Great. Does he know another word? I say, "Yeah. Anyway, I'd still like to see the movie when you're done, Erik."

"First thing tomorrow morning. Or I could bring it by if you need me to," he says. Ms. Miller smiles at his chivalry.

"I'm good," I say. "In fact, I'm *great*. Just *great*."

Ms. Miller clears her throat. "Well, I'm glad you two worked that out then."

As we walk away from Ms. Miller's desk, Erik's eyes narrow and his jaw tightens. I don't think he appreciated my sarcasm.

Jonathon is waiting for me outside class. I intentionally didn't sit anywhere near him in biology.

"Sorry about the chicken thing," he says. "I didn't know it was you."

"What difference does that make?" I say. I know I'm taking out how mad I am at Erik on Jonathon. But neither one of them is my favorite person right now. "When someone's getting creamed, you don't just take a picture of it."

He drops his eyes and his face sags, like he's going to cry. "If I get involved in what I'm filming, it's not honest. It's not art."

"It didn't feel too arty, Jonathon."

"That's what makes it so honest."

I should tell him he smells like stinky socks, but I don't.

He's too sad and I only say things like that on the inside. "Just delete it, okay?"

"I have to be honest, right?"

"Honestly delete it."

"For sure." He looks up. "So do you want to go out, then?"

Even a doormat has to draw a line somewhere. "Honestly. No."

I storm down the hallway of my school wishing I had someone to talk to. I used to. All through grade school and most of junior high I hung out with Danni and Kristi and Annesa. Then Mom got sick and I had to be home to help. Then I started dating Erik and I didn't want to spend a free second on anybody but him. Erik knew everybody and talked enough for both of us. Which was fine with me, or almost fine with me, until Erik stopped talking to me, and now everybody else has too.

So I'm surprised when Sophie Anderson stops me in the hall. Sophie is smart and pretty and is not going to hang around Landon after she graduates, you can just tell. She adjusts her calculus book in her arm and says, "Hey, Myra."

"Hi," I say. She makes me nervous.

She gives me the sweep. "How are you?"

"Good," I say. "How are you?"

"I heard you and Erik broke up."

"Um. Yeah."

Sophie says, "You totally did the right thing. And I don't believe any of those rumors about you anyway."

"What rumors?" I say.

She shrugs. "Oh, don't worry about it. You know how guys are."

"Yeah," I say. I feel like I'm being tackled again.

"I'm just saying . . . he and Ariel and a bunch of people were at my house Saturday night . . . I mean, he acts, like, all sweet, but he isn't, is he? Ariel's bitchy. But Erik gives me the creeps."

I have no idea what to say, so I just stand there. Clearly, I'm a mess.

She puts her hands up and shakes them like they're covered in something disgusting. "I mean *the creeps*! I came upstairs and I heard them in my kitchen. Like *breathing*. In my kitchen. We eat in there. So I made some noise on the stairs. By the time I walked through the entryway Erik was all smiles and Bible stories. He actually asked me about our family's trip to Omaha while he was standing there next to Ariel looking like she'd been mauled by Sasquatch."

Someone else has seen the other side of Erik.

"Sorry," I say.

"Why are you sorry? He's the creep. His mom and my mom are like best friends. They sit around and make humanitarian crap so they can talk about people. You should hear Erik's mom talk about him, like he's the patron saint of good sons. And then he acts like he had to dump you because you can't keep your shirt on." She puts her hand on my arm, but I pull away.

"I gotta go," I say.

I walk away fast. I'm having humiliation whiplash. Two

guys from the track team say hi to me as they pass. Maybe they're just being friendly, but maybe they aren't. I look at them and keep walking.

I cannot graduate fast enough.

The last period of the day I am a TA for sewing. I take roll and then try to sew to calm myself down. I nearly take my finger off in the serger.

Ten minutes later Mrs. Larson, the teacher, says, "They want you down at the office, Myra. And get a bandage on that finger while you're down there."

The main office secretary gives me a smiley face bandage and tells me my mom wants me to call home.

I go out to my car and turn on my cell phone. Mom answers. "I need you to come get us. Melyssa needs to go to her obstetrician."

"Can't you take Melyssa's car?"

"It won't start."

"Can't she wait until after school?"

"No, she can't. She's been throwing up all day."

"You always threw up," I say. It's not that I mind leaving school early. It's that I can't handle one more drama right now.

"And I miscarried a few times, if you'll remember."

"Who's going to get the boys after school?"

"I'll call the school and leave a message for them to wait for you. All you have to do is drop us off. And then you can go get the boys and then come back and get us."

I let my silence register my complaint.

"Do you have any other ideas?" says Mom.

"I'm on my way."

All the way home I am thinking about Erik one second and Melyssa and my mom the next. If I think about being the new school slut, or about Erik and Ariel together, it makes me insane. If I try to focus on Melyssa, I'm flooded with memories of my mother when she was pregnant with my brothers, lying in her bed for months while my dad and I tried to keep everything together, with Melyssa always off being the star of something. I just can't be the nurse again. I look at my finger on the steering wheel. I think I'm going to need a bigger bandage.

When I get to the house, Mel is bad. She's more than pale. You can see the spidery veins in her skin. Mom brings the big plastic bowl that we affectionately call the barf bucket. Just the sight of it makes me ill. Mel gets in the car and cranks up the radio to a station with a guy whining about how bad he wants to jump his girlfriend. Mom says, "Isn't there anything else?"

Mel looks out the window with the bowl bouncing on her knees. No one answers.

I drive as slowly as I can so I won't jiggle her. The road is bumpy to the clinic. Frost heaves.

She says, "If you drive any slower I'll have the baby before we get there."

I speed up. Mel rolls down the window and the icy air slices through the car.

"For heaven's sake," says Mom.

Mel hangs her head out the window.

Mom says, "Can we at least turn that music off? That kind of racket would have made my head fall off when I was pregnant."

"I'm not you," says Mel.

Right as we pull into the parking lot of the clinic, Mel heaves into the bowl. I coast over to the curb. Mel lowers the bowl, rubs her mouth with her sleeve, and says, "That was refreshing."

She puts the bowl on the seat and steps onto the curb, like she's leaving me a loaf of hot bread. Mom gets out too. Mom looks at me with the bowl. "Are you going to survive that?"

"I'll live," I say. "How long are you going to be?"

"We'll do the best we can," says Mom, stiffening. "But you're just going to have to be flexible." She takes Mel's tiny arm. The two of them walk up the stairs and leave me with the bowl.

If I wasn't a germaphobe this would be bad, but for me this bowl might as well be filled with the Ebola virus. Just the smell of it is going to kill me. Being flexible is one thing, balancing a loaded barf bucket while driving is a whole other deal. I try to wedge the bowl against the seat so I can drive to the bushes. It sloshes.

I reach for the hand sanitizer in my glove box. I'm out. How can I be out?

Suddenly I hear my phone ring from inside my purse. I have to touch my purse with germ-covered hands, but I dive in after the sound anyway. I drag out the phone and say, "Hello?"

"Is this Myra Morgan?" says a voice as crisp as starched napkins.

"Yes." I have no idea who this is, but she sounds like she thinks she's important.

"This is Bobbie Hunsaker. Head ranger at the Great Salt Lake State Marina. I understand you are looking for employment."

"Yes," I say. The smell of the bowl is blinding me, but I try to focus. Head ranger?

"Would you be available for an interview Saturday morning after your class meets?"

Why does she know about my class? "That would be terrific."

"I'm looking forward to meeting you."

Just as I am trying to find a way to ask her how she knows so much about me, there is a tapping at my window. Much to my horror, it's a police officer with surprisingly hairy knuckles. I have no idea what I've done. I roll down the window.

He starts to talk and then makes a gagging face. He stares at the barf bucket. "You're in the red zone, young lady. That's not allowed." He looks at the bucket again. "Unless you need me to move the car for you."

I say, "I'll move." Then I remember I still have a phone at the side of my face.

"Sounds like you're busy," says Bobbie Hunsaker. Her voice is pressed and puckered.

I look at the policeman but answer the phone. "Sort of."

"Well, see you Saturday?"

"I'll be there," I say.

I close the phone as the policeman disappears into my rearview mirror.

I turn the car on using as few fingers as possible. It's important to contain the germs. I tell myself I'm two minutes from a bathroom where I can lose the bowl. I can do this. *GERMS BAD BUT REMOVABLE.* Then I look down at my dashboard and realize I'm almost out of gas. The policeman sits in his car and watches me pull away from the curb.

I drive in circles around the parking lot until the policeman leaves. Then I slowly pull over to a garbage can and put the entire evil bowl into the can. It makes a loud spilling sound. Normally I would lose my mind at the thought that I have filled this can with a repulsive liquid that will probably never be washed out and that I have wasted a perfectly good plastic bowl. But not today. Today I'm an illegally parking, bad daughter with barf on her hands.

I know I'm going to catch it from my mom later when she can't find the bowl, but I don't care. I really don't. As I drive away from the garbage, I feel better, and it's not just because the stench is gone.

I roll down the windows with my pinkie finger, which I'm pretty sure is clean, and let the fresh air into the car. Maybe doing the wrong thing for the right reasons is better than doing the right thing for the wrong reasons. At least it feels that way. Now all I need is a gas station, hand sanitizer, a thousand dollars, and a brilliant research proposal.

I'll start with the gas station.

# 16

## Down Feathers:
*The short fluffy ones that keep birds warm.*

It's late, really late, when Carson sneaks down to see me. I am reading about the Galápagos cormorants' mating dance, which starts with them swimming around each other with their necks in a swan-style S, then taking themselves up onto the shore and interlocking their necks and making these low guttural sounds in their throats. Then they twirl around until they get riled up enough to go for it. For birds it sounds kind of, well, you know—so I nearly jump out of my sleeping bag when I hear Carson's voice behind me. "Are you down here because you're mad at Melyssa?"

Once I get my wits back I say, "I'm not mad."

The truth is I've spent most of the night (up until I was reading bird porn) in a frozen rage at my mom and sister. I know it makes more sense to hate Erik, but it's harder. There are so many good days with Erik I have to forget. And part of me wonders, in a deeply ironic way, if he did dump me because

I'm destined to get pregnant without a permit. My mom (not that he knows about her) and my sister both did. Maybe I am from a long line of knocked-up women and I don't even know it. Maybe my DNA has an extra baby-making bump.

Carson says, "You can sleep in my room. It's warmer."

"I like it down here." I pull Carson under the blanket with me. We kick our toes around until both our legs are covered. We look up at the plastic green stars I thumbtacked to the bare beams. "I've been reading this cool book about a place where animals aren't afraid of people. Even the birds."

"Is it real? Or in your story?"

"Both. They have birds and lizards that swim."

"Dinosaurs?"

"Pretty close."

"Can we go there?"

"It's real but it's out in the middle of the ocean. For a long time only missionaries and pirates went to these islands. Even now it's pretty hard to get there."

"That sucks," says Carson.

"Don't say 'sucks,'" I say.

Upstairs I can hear my parents talking. Occasionally I hear my dad's low tones, but mostly my mother's wordless voice cuts through the floor until the furnace goes on and drowns them out.

Carson gloms on to me. "I miss you." His voice is sleepy and warm.

"You can't miss me. I'm right here."

"You seem far away."

I look up at my green stars and thaw a little. "Do you want to sleep down here tonight?"

He twists onto his side and then rolls back over again.

He rubs his toes against my shins. They are like ten little icicles. "Do you want to go up to your own bed?"

"Yeah." He gets up to go. He's delirious. "Are you going to stay down here forever?"

"Just until things settle down."

"Settle down to what?"

"I don't know," I say. "To something else."

"Don't leave, okay?"

"Who said I was leaving?" I say.

After Carson's gone I turn out the light and close my eyes. I've decided the dark is the worst place after a breakup. In the dark I can see the past. I can remember what it used to be like to have someone hold me. I can see Erik leaning back against his truck, shivering in the cold, so I could wear his coat while we stood in my driveway and talked. What I loved about Erik at those wonderful moments was not who he was but how he made me feel. When I was with him it seemed like anything could happen.

I guess something did happen, just not what I wanted.

I force myself to think of cormorants. I figure that will put me to sleep at least. I imagine them twirling, neck and neck. But soon my mind drifts, and I see the thin brown birds standing on the turquoise shore, drying their tiny flightless feathers in the ocean wind, so far from the pirate ship marooned on Deadendia's sad shores.

# 17

# Spur:
*A bone that pokes out of birds' feet,
for fighting dirty.*

Erik calls at five on Thursday night.

I look at the number. I let it ring four times. Why is he calling? Five times. I can't stand it. I pick up.

He says, "Sorry to bother you."

"You aren't bothering me," I say. Long awkward pause.

"I think I left one of my track sweatshirts over at your house. The one with the pirate on it."

"Oh," I say. Pirates are Cyprus High's mascot, but suddenly the guy with the knife in his teeth seems like the perfect emblem for Erik.

"Yeah, well, can you bring it to school on Monday? We're wearing 'em for a meet on Tuesday."

I imagine myself giving back the sweatshirt in front of the entire track team, including Ariel. I say, "Or you could just come get it."

"I don't need it until Tuesday. Just bring it to school," he says.

*Don't be a doormat, don't be a doormat, don't be a doormat.* Returning clothes to your rumor-spreading ex in the hall is worse than being a doormat. I say, "I'll bring it in my car. You can come grab it after school." That's reasonable. Unemotional.

There's another awkward pause. "It's not going to make a difference," he says. "I wish you'd stop trying to make this into something."

I'm stunned. "You called me."

"For my sweatshirt," he says.

"It'll be on the curb. Next to the trash cans." I clamp my phone shut.

In five minutes I have his rotten pirate sweatshirt in an apple box with every other piece of Erik junk I can find. Stuffed animals, a T-shirt that never fit right, dance pictures, photo booth pictures, cinnamon gum, dried flowers, pink socks, two pairs of earrings, matchbooks, and three boxes of stale, crappy chocolate. I unpair the socks.

I walk out to the curb. I stand there for a second and then I drop the box. Not by accident. I open my arms and let it fall. Which is utterly cool until the box hits the ground and a picture frame breaks and sends a shard of glass flying past my head, just missing my face. I have nearly blinded myself with a dance photo.

I get a broom and a dustpan. Then I sweep up the nearly invisible flakes of glass and dump them back into the box on top of the sweatshirt.

The next morning my dad goes out for the paper and

comes back with Ms. Miller's Galápagos DVD. "I found this on the driveway. You know anything about it?" He tosses it on the kitchen table.

I stare at the dirt-smudged movie case. "A friend from my study group must have dropped it off," I say. "I'm writing a paper about the Galápagos."

"That's pretty careless. I could have run it over."

I wish I'd thrown Erik's stuff into the street.

In biology we talk about parasites. Which is about as repulsive as it gets. I answer three questions in a row about built-in defense systems and freak Ms. Miller out. Erik answers two questions and he gets one wrong. She sticks her hands in her lab coat and stares at me. "Myra Morgan, you've been holding out on me."

Who knew there were 342 parasites that can live on or in humans? Me, that's who. Because after Erik tossed the DVD on my driveway I snuggled up to my biology textbook and studied my brains out. I'm no genius, but I can memorize. And I've been typing Erik's essays up since we started dating. So I guess the last nineteen months aren't a total loss.

After class Jonathon asks me if I want to go see *Dead Man's Daughter*. "You can practically smell it."

I say, "Thanks. But I have work to do."

# 18

# Niche:

*When a bird finds just the right place so it won't
starve or get munched.*

Saturday morning my alarm goes off in my dreams, but I
don't wake up at first, I just dream about a jackhammer going
off on the basement floor. When I do finally wake up I slam
my hand into my alarm and realize I have five minutes to
get ready for class and my interview. I race upstairs, throwing on lights and opening drawers in the bathroom. Melyssa
stumbles into the bathroom scowling.

She hangs on to the door frame to steady herself. "You
have got to be the noisiest human being in the world."

"Sorry. I'm late."

"Why are you doing your makeup then? To impress
Prince Charming? Like he's going to care. Look at you. You're
anorexic."

"Did you borrow my new lipstick?"

"He's a self-centered, hypocritical weasel."

I brush by her into the hall. "I've been saving it."

Mel wanders back to her room. Over her shoulder she says, "You're pathetic."

"I have an interview," I say, but she isn't listening. Her door is already shut.

I am late to class, but so is Pete.

There are a lot fewer kids than the last time we met. The Galápagos cheer must not have been enough to inspire all the other geniuses to get out of bed and do more unassigned homework. Or maybe the competition seemed too steep. My guess is the really smart kids are the ones home in bed. We're down to me, Erik, Pritchett (the pain), Dawn (the goth), Ho-Bong and Ho-Jun (the superconductor twins), and one Megan. We all stand out in the cold under the streetlight, rubbing our hands, waiting for Pete to show up. I stand alone and look down. Then I see Erik's shiny white tennis shoes practically on top of my black flats. I can smell the soap on his skin.

"You're looking nice," Erik says. The sarcasm is so faint it's hard to be sure of.

I look up at his face and he smiles. Even at an obscene hour my stomach reflexively flips at that stupid smile. Maybe I shouldn't have exploded his stuff on the curb.

"Hi," I say. I guess I can pretend he didn't throw the DVD under my dad's car too.

He smiles again. I almost believe he means it. It must be the glare from his teeth.

"So you going somewhere today?" he says.

"I have a job interview." Everyone can hear what we're saying, so I don't exactly want to talk about it.

"At the harbor?" He laughs softly. "Doing what?"

I say, "I'm applying for secretary." My words snap on the end of my tongue.

"Oh yeah? That'll be perfect for you." Erik's genius is keeping his own hands clean while he gets everyone else's dirty. Or maybe his genius is being a genius and being dirty is just a hobby.

"Thanks," I say. Maybe I go a little overboard on the bitter tone in my voice.

Everyone is listening now. To the sound of hate-your-guts silence. Until Pete steps into the ring and says, "Good morning, everyone. Sorry I'm late."

No one talks.

Pete says, "Did I miss something?"

When we get inside Pete says, "What do you geniuses know about Darwin?"

Nobody moves. It's a trick question.

Finally Pritchett says, "He spent a few weeks in the Galápagos and then he spent the rest of his life making bank on it. Cha-ching."

I'm starting to think this kid is a plant for a reality TV show.

Pete moves to the back of the room and sets up a projector with his laptop. He shoots a picture onto the wall and hits the lights. The photo is of a white one-story building in a tropical location. Once he gets everything in focus we can see that it's the Charles Darwin Research Center, and Pete is standing out in front of the center with a tall man, probably in his fifties, and a blonde woman in red shorts. Pritchett whistles through his teeth—at the woman, I'm assuming. Pete's hair is longer and his skin is dark brown. He looks more like a surfer than a biologist. I get the funny feeling again.

"This is the building where we rendezvous with other biologists on the trip."

"How come you aren't going this time?" says Dawn.

"The committee decided it was better the grad students took turns going. I'll get down there again soon."

For some reason it blows me away to see someone who I kind of know standing in this place. To me it's like somebody showing a slide show of their road trip to heaven, and then talking about going back and forth like it's a trip to the car wash.

"Sweet tan," says Erik.

"Believe me, the tan is the least of things that are sweet in the Galápagos, but let's get back to Darwin and the project. Everything is hypercontrolled on the islands now. The Ecuadorians don't want people coming in and raiding the place like the bad old days."

Ho-Bong says, "Why is their research center named after an Englishman then?"

"Great question," says Pete. "The center isn't named after Darwin because he was the only person who ever discovered anything important on the Galápagos, or because he was the first guy to put his mitts on the theory of evolution. The center is named after him because he wasn't about 'cha-ching,' for the most part. Like many men of his age—sorry, ladies, women mostly weren't included back then—he was a scientist, with human flaws that kept getting in his way. But Darwin was in it for the long haul, even if he didn't know it when he came to the islands. In fact, I think it's safe to say he had no idea what he'd found until he was on the boat home.

"Darwin was there to look at volcanoes and funky rocks. But he couldn't leave the animals alone. So he started collecting all kinds of stuff out of sheer curiosity. Among other things he collected four birds on four islands. On his way home he started to realize that the birds were more important than he'd assumed. Each bird could be identified by its island, its origin. That's when the homework started."

Pete flashes a quote on the wall: "It is the fate of every voyager, when he has just discovered what object in any place is more particularly worthy of his attention, to be hurried from it. Charles Darwin."

"I don't get it," says Dawn.

"That's good," says Pete. "That means you're actually thinking about it."

Ho-Bong and Ho-Jun speak in Korean to each other, but everyone else is quiet. It seems like they talk a long time.

Finally Pete says, "So guys, wanna share your opinions with the class?"

I can't see Ho-Bong's face in the dark, but his voice is suddenly flat and American. "We never know what we're looking for until we aren't there anymore."

After class I go out in the hall. For some reason Darwin's quote is stuck in my head, like some sort of philosophical earworm. I look up from my deep thoughts to see a heavyset woman wearing a shirt that has the insignia DNR on the arm, which I'm hoping stands for "Division of Natural Resources," not "Do Not Resuscitate." She's sitting at the front desk, checking her watch. The interview. I totally forgot.

She has red hair bobbed at her ears and freckles everywhere, even on her eyelids, but she looks all business, which is not how the rest of the room looks. The desk is buried in papers. The surrounding room is dusty and has a noticeable scent of mold.

I walk to the front desk. "Are you Ms. Hunsaker?"

"You must be Myra. Just call me Ranger Bobbie."

She has long arms for a woman. I try to be mature and stick my hand out to shake hers.

She grabs my hand and squeezes the blood out of it. "Are you honest?"

"Yes."

"Are you organized?"

"Yes."

"On a scale of one to ten, how reliable are you?"

"Nine."

"Really? How did you like my handshake?"

I look her right in the freckles. "It hurt."

She smiles. "You'll do."

"I'll do what?" I ask.

Ranger Bobbie hands me a bright orange piece of paper. "You're hired."

I look at the paper. It's an employment application. "I don't even know what the job is."

"Well, sure. I'm sorry I'm in a bit of a rush today so I'll make this quick. Some joker tried to get his boat out of the dock when the water was too low in the launch and now we're going to have to tow him. Anyway, your end of it is I need this whole place organized. Files, supplies, everything. Answer the phone. Tell people to go to the Web site for prices on boat slips, that kind of thing. We're closed at five every day. Mainly I want you to clean this place up. We're a year-round facility, but in the wintertime everything goes to pot." Her face is tight and worn. She sighs. "I cover everything from the west desert, the whole stinking lake, all the way to the city limits. I barely have time to overeat." She pats her well-padded waist.

I stand there looking stupid, but I like her.

"Anyway, this is a poorly paid part-time position. But Peter says you're desperate."

"I am." Pete thinks I'm *desperate*? I hand her a list of the times I can work if I drop out of sewing and get early release. "But these are the only hours I can work while I'm still in school."

She reads over my sheet. "This will be fine for a few months."

"Don't you want to see my résumé?"

"Your dad hired a nephew of mine at the plant. My nephew says he's never seen a man who is more fair and hard-working. Does the apple fall far from that tree?"

"Which apple?"

"Are you a hard worker, like your dad?"

"Yes."

"I trust you can file in alphabetical order and run a computer better than I can."

I nod, trying to keep up.

"Are you good on a computer?"

"I'm okay."

"Fine. This desk is your first item of business. The guy running this office right now is a total slob. And there he is now." She stands to go.

Pete walks toward us. "That's a little harsh."

Ranger Bobbie says, "Good grief, Pete. Can't you even throw junk mail away? This place is a disgrace."

"I was getting around to it."

She points a long finger at my job description. "Okay, enough. So here are the things I want you to do. Here's the filing cabinet. Here's the computer. Pete can tell you the passwords. Every once in a while they'll need you as a spare body for some search-and-rescue stuff."

"Search and rescue?"

"Oh, people are always falling in the icy water at the most inconvenient times and places. But don't worry. We have Pete and a few other crusty types to help us with that."

"Okay," I say.

"We'll start you at minimum and begrudgingly give you a raise about the time you find something better to do with your life. If you do a good job for us, you can work more after you graduate. Summer gets busy. You have any questions?"

"What am I doing again?"

"You'll figure it out. Don't let Pete con you into doing his laundry, if he has any. Don't be a doormat to him. He'll just walk all over you, if you know what I mean?"

I nod. Doormat. Sheez. Do I have WELCOME written on my forehead?

"One more thing," says Ranger Bobbie. "Nobody eats the mocha almond fudge out of the freezer." She glares at Pete. I almost laugh, but she looks serious.

"I don't know who'd do that," says Pete.

"I mean it," says Bobbie. "Things have been known to happen out on that lake to employees caught stealing."

"Aye, aye, cap'n," says Pete.

# 19

## Incubation:
### *Sitting on an egg so the bird inside stays warm enough to keep growing.*

When I get home I hear the cement mixer in the backyard. My mother's concrete dreams are coming true. Who said there isn't fun after forty?

My brothers are waiting at the door. "You gotta get us to hoops right now. Mom's mad."

I walk into the backyard. Dad and Mom are hard at work pouring. Danny is off getting covered in mud in the corner of the yard.

Dad is lost in a world of perfect measurements and standards of engineering excellence. Mom straightens up her back slowly and comes over, away from the mixer. She has a glob of wet cement in her hair that blends with her gray. She yells over the noise, "Where've you been?"

I yell back, "I got a new job."

"I thought you were studying for a test."

I yell, "I'm going to be a secretary at the marina."

"The marina?" Mom motions me farther away from the cement mixer so we can talk normally, or as normally as my mother and I ever talk. She says, "You got a job at the lake? They found a woman who'd been set on fire down there two weeks ago."

"They did?" I say. "I didn't hear about that."

"There are a lot of things you don't hear about when you're in high school. I'm glad you got a job, but how are you going to be a secretary when you're in class all day?"

Across the muddy lawn, Danny is crawling on his knees to get a ball that has gone into a bush. He's going to rip those jeans for sure, and probably rip up his knees while he's at it. All Dad would have to do is look up and tell Danny to stand over the bush to get the ball.

I look back at Mom. "I'm going to take work release instead of sewing. I can work every other day and weekends until five."

"Who's going to watch the kids between four-thirty and five-thirty when I leave and you get home?"

I knew this would make her mad. "Andrew knows how to babysit."

Mom looks at me skeptically. "He's eleven."

"I was taking care of the boys at nine. And Mel will be here. It's only for an hour, every other day, and I'll put the food for dinner together the night before so all I'll have to do when I get home is put it in the oven."

"Who's going to bring the kids home from school on those days?"

I give her a pleading look.

"So I'm going to have to drive the carpool when I'm trying to get things together here before work." She sighs. "Is it a good job at least?"

"Mostly I'm organizing things right now, during the slow season. But they might bring me on full-time and then I'd make more. I could borrow Melyssa's car to take the kids in the morning on the days I work, so you'd have Moby and . . . I'd be back before you left. And I'd still do dinner and clean up every night."

"Oh, fine. I don't have anything else to do right before I go to work all night, right?" She smiles. I know she's not happy, but at least she's willing to try it out. "If this doesn't work you'll quit, right?"

"Right." I hug her stiffly. It really is cool of her.

Brett and Andrew stand close by. "Could we stop the hugging and start the driving?" Andrew asks.

"Like yesterday," says Brett.

A yell erupts from the center of the yard. It's not Danny. It's Dad. Danny has thrown a basketball in the middle of Dad's perfectly level cement. Dad looks like someone just stepped on his birthday cake. Andrew and Brett crack up. Okay, I do too.

Dad throws his hands in the air at us. "That was perfectly good cement. What is wrong with this family?"

"There's a list," Mom mutters.

～～～～～

By nightfall, I've been to two basketball games, cleaned the house, made brownies, and redecorated the basement in the shabby-no-seriously-shabby look. It's amazing what a shelf, an old rug, a heating lamp, and a door propped up on food storage containers can do to spruce up a dungeon.

I sit in the light of my lamp and pore over my books on the Galápagos Islands and cormorants. It doesn't feel like homework. It's more like torture. I wonder what I'm doing. I can fake my way through a test if I need to. But my idea of creativity is putting sour cream in the frosting. There is no way I can come up with a proposal better than Erik's or those other brains'. And then there's that whole issue of the thousand dollars.

I open the book Pete has given me. The turquoise eyes of the cormorant, matching the turquoise sky, look back at me.

> With fewer than fifteen hundred currently in existence, the exquisite flightless cormorant is a rare jewel indeed, perhaps one of the rarest birds in the world. Found only off the shores of Isabela and Fernandina islands, the flightless cormorant has evolved into a lovely example of natural peculiarity.
>
> Although one might at first pity the creature for its puny wings, the birds are well suited to their particular biological niche. Heavy and powerful, these birds dive into the turbulent coastal waters like feather-lined torpedoes. Their small wings carry

fewer water bubbles than those of their flying relatives, thus creating less resistance.

They are also quite fertile when necessary. This pliability preserves the species in times of disease or environmental calamity. For obvious reasons, they rarely travel far from where they are born.

I like this bird less and less the more I read about it. What is Pete thinking?

My brothers all come rumbling down the stairs. Since it's Saturday night they're all up late looking to break some heads or at least toilet paper something. "Hey!" yells Andrew. "What are you doing?"

"Studying," I say.

They all four climb on my sleeping bag, with me in it, to get warm. It kind of hurts, but I love being buried in brothers.

"It's creepy down here," says Brett.

"I know," says Andrew. "Can I move down here when you move out?"

"Why should you get it all to yourself?" says Brett.

I wiggle free and sit up. "Did the TV upstairs break or something?"

"We want to know what happens to the pirates," says Danny.

"And the prince," says Carson.

"What about the scullery maid?" I say.

They all look at me blankly.

"Okay. When last we saw the sad inhabitants of Dead-endia, they were listening to the pirate king tell his wild tales of the island of Isabela, with the promise that this faraway place held a jewel so magical that it could stop evil trolls in their tracks."

"And some of them wanted to go get it," says Carson.

"Only two would have the honor and the curse to travel to Isabela. The competition to sail would be as fierce as the honor would be great. First they would have to win a wrestling match. The rules were simple: The last man standing was the winner. The competition was more complicated: The wrestling match was against a pirate that was half donkey."

"Which half?" says Andrew.

"He looked mostly like a man, but he had the brain and strength of a donkey. He wore a magically strong red bandanna over his donkey ears, and he won all his fights by knocking people down when they weren't looking. One by one, six would-be travelers fell to his brutal head butts, until at last it was a scullery maid's turn. All the other fair maidens had chickened out, but not this one. She had chickened in."

"What?" say the boys.

"It just so happened that the scullery maid had fried some chicken the night before, and it smelled delicious. When it was her turn she simply went to her rucksack and unwrapped the chicken in front of the famished donkey man. He sat right down and began eating before he realized he had left her standing and victorious."

"That's cheating," Andrew says.

"No," I say, "it's adapting."

"Is that the only test?" says Brett.

"No, there are two more. The second test was that they had to give up ten gold coins."

"Why?"

"Pirates like treasure."

"So what did the scullery maid do for that?" says Andrew.

"She lost. The prince and a really tall court jester were better financed."

"What was the third test?" says Brett. He looks bored.

"The ghost chest. Haunted by spirits of birds that die alone and miserable at sea, its glittering, gory loot can only be recovered if the chest is unlocked with bird language. If the travelers couldn't speak to the cormorants, there would be no point in going."

"Bird language?" says Andrew. "What is it with you and birds?"

"Like, who's going to know that?" says Brett, shaking his head.

"Most pirates speak bird," says Carson.

Danny asks, "So who wins?"

"None of them. They all had to learn."

"Why not just get the pirates to do it for them?" says Danny.

We all look at Danny.

"Good question," I say. "But only the true seeker of the magic stone can command it."

"Whatever," says Brett.

# 20

# Cavity Nests:
*Nests in trees or holes. Safer but stuffy.*

My first day of work is Monday after school. When I get to the marina office, it's locked. I step back from the window, wondering what I should do. I walk outside and look around. The masts of the boats tip in the wind. The state flag flaps hard. A storm must be on its way. A gull passes over me. I wave. It squawks.

I stand on the sidewalk. I mumble to myself, "Doesn't anybody keep track of things around here?"

Pete comes out of the women's restroom, holding a wrench and a pipe that is dripping something. "Hey, you're here."

"Yeah," I say, trying not to look at the pipe.

He laughs and twirls the pipe once, but it falls out of his hand and lands on the ground with a clank. After he picks it up he laughs again. "Pretty much do everything around here, whether I know what I'm doing or not."

"Yeah," I say profoundly. I'm suddenly a bag of nerves being alone with Pete. He's someplace weird in my head. Not my age. Not a grown-up. Not ugly enough. But with really germy hands.

After he unlocks the office, we go inside and survey the mess. Let's say it's impressive.

Pete says, "So I have to go up to school now. The university, I mean. You have any questions?"

"You're leaving?" I say. I try to override my panic button. "What am I supposed to do?"

"Just kind of organize things. Make Bobbie happy. Answer the phone if it rings."

"What do I say?"

"Hello?" he says, walking toward a camper.

"What if they ask me something?"

"Bobbie left you a sheet. It's on my desk somewhere. It has the hours and the rules. You could probably read that."

Why is it that adults are always giving me a job and then walking off before they explain what I'm supposed to do?

He keeps talking like I'm following him, which I'm not. "And put up a sign, would you? Restroom is closed for today."

"I'll do a better job if you show me where to put things."

He says, "That's assuming I know where things go."


When I open the first file-cabinet drawer in the office I find ten pounds of paper, a squeaky dog toy, and a half-eaten bag of Tootsie Rolls. There are receipts, invoices, and Victoria's Secret catalogs all mixed together. I burst out laughing.

"What's so funny?" says Pete.

I startle. "You're still here?"

"I thought I'd better show you the trash heap and all."

"How do you know where anything is?"

"I just find it when I need it," says Pete.

"But what about the bills getting paid?"

"We had someone doing that. But she quit."

"How do you do all your stuff for school and work here?"

"I'm researching my dissertation right now, so I only have to teach one class this semester. I live here, so it doesn't take up that much extra time some days."

"You live here?"

"I live in the camper. Weird, huh?"

I shrug my shoulders. "I live in my parents' unfinished basement in a sleeping bag."

"Sounds like me at your age."

Except for the beard, Pete looks like he could be my age. I say, "Is getting your PhD a killer?"

"School's easy. It's jumping through all their hoops that slows me down. Arrested development, I guess. Do you need anything before I go?"

I lift the lid on a prehistoric box of donuts poking out from under a stack of newspapers. I may have found the epicenter of the mold. "Because you know where it is?"

"Good point," says Pete.

I stack and sort and chuck for two hours. At four o'clock I get a call on my cell. It's Andrew.

"I'm not sure where Danny is!"

I remind myself to breathe. "What? How long has he been missing?"

"I'm not sure. He was playing hide-and-seek with Carson and then Carson couldn't find him."

"Where's Melyssa?"

"Asleep. Mom told me not to wake her up unless it was an emergency."

"Okay. Let's try something first. Were they playing inside or out?"

"In."

"Okay. Did you look in all the hampers and the cupboards? Start with the hamper in their room."

Andrew leaves the phone and comes back. "Got him."

I say, "Just hold on to him until Dad shows up."

There's no sign of Ranger Bobbie. When the marina phone rings, I read the info sheet Bobbie left for me. At one point an old guy shuffles in to ask for Pete and then scowls at me. He says, "You doing this permanent?"

"Not sure."

"You don't look too old."

"I'm not."

"I give you two weeks, tops." He looks at me, waiting for me to argue.

"Why only two?"

"You'll find out."

He shuffles back out and turns to scowl at me again as he walks away.

My cell goes off. "How's the new job?" says Dad. He's calling from the house.

"Why are you home so early?" I say. "Did Andrew lose Danny again?"

"Again? Danny's fine. You going to be there all day?"

"I work until five."

"If I feed the boys, do you think you could take Melyssa out?"

"Does she want to go out?" Mel yelled at everyone in the house before I'd finished making pancakes this morning.

Dad says, "You don't need to take her bowling. Just get her out of the house for a few hours."

I have a ton of reading to do on my proposal and an English lit test in the morning. Not to mention that Mel told me I was a self-righteous Betty Crock-of-Crap when I asked her to stop yelling at Brett for giving her the silent treatment. I say, "I thought she was supposed to rest."

"Carson is threatening to run away from home."

"Gotcha," I say.


I take Mel to the Hungry Horse steak house. Her idea. Dad's money. There's a line out the door.

"You sure you want to wait in this line?" I say.

Mel pulls Dad's T-shirt down over her stretchy jeans. "What else do I have to do tonight?"

"You're going to be on your feet."

"Oh, please. You're as bad as Mom. I'm not going to keel over from standing up."

I go to the counter to put our name on the waiting list. A girl who graduated from my high school a year ago is the hostess. She's thin and blonde and supposedly did the whole basketball team. We've never spoken.

"I need a seat for two."

"Is an hour going to be okay for ya?"

"Not really," I say. "Could you seat us at the bar faster?"

"Help yourself," the girl says, and then loses all interest in me.

I get Melyssa and we sit down at the bar. A bald bartender in his twenties comes over to us. He focuses on Mel's stomach. "I'm sorry, ladies, we can't serve you here."

"Hey, Steve," says Melyssa unhappily. "It's me, Melyssa Morgan."

The bald guy looks carefully at my swollen sister. "No shit." Then instantly looks embarrassed. "It is you."

"No shit," says Mel. "You can serve us. We aren't going to drink. Not tonight, anyway."

He does the eye shift thing for a minute. "Yeah, I think that's all right. How you been, Mel? I thought you were off at college getting famous or something."

"I went with 'or something.' How you been, Steve?"

"Good. Well, sort of. Working here at night and for my dad in the day. Me and Hally just had our first kid six months ago."

"Congrats. Girl or boy?"

"Boy. Hally would get a kick out of seeing you. You and your hubby should come by."

"No hubby."

He rubs the mug he's holding with a bar towel. "Wow. Sorry, Mel. It happens, man. It happens."

"Apparently," says Mel. "How are the cheese fries?"

A waitress eventually shuttles us to a booth after Steve puts a word in for us. By the time we've eaten, three women from town have come over to wish Melyssa a happy baby. She's about as friendly with them as she was with Steve.

"Why do you do that?" I say after the last woman leaves to go back to her booth with her tail between her legs. "They're just trying to be nice."

"Do you think so?" says Melyssa. "Or maybe they're just rubbing my face in it."

"She was just being nice."

She eats another cheese fry. "If you believe that, you're as stupid as they are."

"Probably," I say. "And you're probably better at taking tests and writing papers than most of the people in this restaurant. Maybe most of the people in this town, except Dad."

"If I have to live in this town for another six months, I'm going to lose my mind."

"Maybe. But that doesn't make you smarter."

Melyssa scans the crowd. I watch her eyeball all the baseball caps and overprocessed hair. "You're so trapped in this hole you don't even know how bad it is."

"If it's so bad, why'd you come back?"

"I'm broke and pregnant, in case you hadn't noticed."

"You could have stayed with Zeke."

Melyssa sits back in her seat and sizes me up. I guess she's not used to the doormat asking questions. "He moved out, remember?"

"Only after you told him he was a loser," I say.

"Look." She stares past me, done with my little sister commentary. "If I make mistakes they're my mistakes. I'm not trying to please anyone or buy into anyone else's idea of what's right, including Zeke."

"So why'd you get pregnant with him?"

Melyssa doesn't answer for a few seconds. She's counting baseball caps again. "It happens."

# 21

# Screech:

*A group of gulls. Not just the sound they make.*

"Today we're going to take a field trip to Antelope Island. This is going to take a few hours. Everyone up for that?" Pete looks at me. It makes me feel like such a project. I nod. He looks around the rest of the class, minus the last Megan. We're becoming endangered applicants.

"You're going to want to bundle up in the blankets I keep in the van. It's breezy."

We pile in. There are three seat belts and two moth-eaten blankets. The seats are ripped in two places with the stuffing bulging out. The whole van reeks of french fries. Pritchett says, "Nice ride," as he grabs one of the blankets. Dawn gets the other one and they both move to the back. Erik gets in with them. I'm sandwiched between the twins in the middle row. I get a loose seat-cushion spring in my backside to keep me warm. I could sit up front with Pete, but he has his equipment stacked on the seat and I'm trying not to be the teacher's pet/project.

"Fuel inefficient," says Ho-Jun to his brother over the top of me. I realize it's the first time I've heard him speak in English, except to say his name, which isn't in English, but at least I know what it means.

Pete leans back. "It runs on grease."

"That explains the smell," Pritchett says. "Or almost explains it."

Ho-Bong says, "How many miles per gallon?"

"Sixty, some days," says Pete.

I try squeezing my butt so I won't feel the spring as much. Ho-Bong gives me a sideways stare.

"Yep, it's a sweet ride," says Pete. "I go by the Chicken Little Drive-Thru every weekend and fill up. They don't charge me anything. I guess it cuts down on their waste output."

"That's disgusting," says Dawn.

For the next half hour, we drive while Pete explains alternative fuels over the bang of his engine. Only Ho-Bong and Ho-Jun look interested. But Pete chatters on like he's telling us the plot of a sex-driven murder mystery. I try to listen, but between the piece of metal jamming in my rear and freezing to death, I have a hard time concentrating. I look back once and see Erik texting. I know there is an exhibition track meet today. This class must really be cutting into his Ariel time.

When we get to the causeway, the island looks bleak and barren. The sulfur stench of the low tide competes with the rotten smell in the car. The gray sky blends with the water and dull hills of the island. I've been to Antelope Island before, so I know what's here—a few trapped buffalo and antelope and a whole lot of nothing else.

As soon as we pass over the causeway, Pete stops talking about engines. "Everybody get to a window and stick out your hand. Hurry up."

We all look at each other.

"Come on," says Pete. "I'm going to give you a flying lesson."

We push around each other and stick our arms out of the cranked windows. I wedge myself on the floor and lean out. It's not comfortable.

"Now make your hand like a wing and surf the current. Hopefully you've done this before."

I angle my hand like a plane in takeoff, then bend it in and out of the wind. The speed of the van makes the air bitter cold, but at least I'm not sitting on the spring.

Pete shouts over the engine and the wind. "This is thrust. A bird flies by moving forward with strong muscles and a light, aerodynamic body. But they also need lift. That's when the bird sets its wings in such a way that air can't flow through them and the airflow on top is faster than underneath, making the bird rise. Hollow bones and hinged, multipurpose feathers were some important adaptations that probably allowed birds to survive when their prehistoric buddies were dropping like stones."

"So we can't fly because we're fat and don't have wings?" says Dawn.

"Not fat so much as heavy. We'd also need gigantic chest muscles, hollow bones, and a bigger heart. But there's always evolution, baby."

"How about buying a plane ticket?" says Erik.

Pete says, "That's probably fastest."

I keep my hand moving in the wind.

We drive to a lookout point and emerge from the van. Pete jumps out ahead of us and hands out a brochure-looking thing along with tiny pencils. "Here is your birding list for the birds you are likely to see in the Great Salt Lake and the surrounding area. Every time you see one of these birds, you check it off."

I look through the columns of bird names. There must be two hundred birds listed. Ruby-crowned kinglet, sharp-shinned hawk, pine siskin, canvasback, Lapland larkspur, willet, and black-chinned hummingbird. Birds I have never heard of before, and they live in, or at least they travel through, my backyard.

Pete starts talking in his National Geographic baritone. "The stinky, salinated water you see before you is the life-blood of this state's ecology and the four to six million birds that migrate through here every year. It makes up eighty percent of Utah's wetlands. It creates the weather for the Wasatch Front, better known to the locals as the lake effect. In addition to bison, mule deer, bighorn sheep, pronghorn, and antelope, there are two hundred and fifty different species of birds and plenty of insects in and out of the water for all the birds to eat. Some people call this America's Dead

Sea, but as you can see, there is nothing dead about it."

Behind me I hear Dawn say, "Could it be any colder out here?"

Pete keeps lecturing. "This time of year we can see California gulls, of course, those recycling beauties, but also bald eagles, winter ducks, and prairie falcons."

"Where are the cormorants?" I ask.

"Probably not going to see any cormorants, at least not for a few weeks. They need the ice off the freshwater. Plus they like to tan in Belize."

"Well, who wouldn't," mumbles Dawn.

Two hundred and fifty species of birds fly through this airspace and he suggests a bird to me that doesn't even check in until my proposal is practically due? I'm not actually writing on this kind of cormorant . . . but still.

Pete looks at me. "Don't look so sad, Myra. You can still write about the ones in Ecuador."

"Thanks," I say. I don't mean to sound sarcastic, I just feel that way.

After we spot an ibis and are mobbed by five gulls, we get back in the unmagical school bus and head down the road to a tiny outcropping. We pile out into a parking lot surrounded by large boulders, which I assume are supposed to be like a seawall. The rocks may keep the parking lot from going in a storm, but they don't keep out the wind or the spraying water. It's freezing.

Pete climbs the rocks like a mountain goat. When he's on top he yells, "Straight ahead, Egg Island!"

Nobody moves toward the rock Pete's posing on. It looks cold up there with the wind blowing and the water spraying.

Erik says, "This guy drinks way too much coffee."

"Too much sumpin'," says Pritchett, pinching his fingers together like he's smoking.

Erik shakes his head. "Sure glad I'm missing a meet for this crap."

Ho-Jun and Ho-Bong nod in agreement. Ho-Bong says, "We're missing baseball. And our coach takes it out of our butts."

Dawn looks at Pritchett. "What team are you on, big guy?"

"I'm on my own team, small-town white girl," says Pritchett.

"Sorry," says Dawn, going pink in her ghostly cheeks.

Pete yells above us. "Don't leave me hanging!"

I bolt for the rocks with Ho-Bong and Ho-Jun right behind me. All this peer bonding is making me crazy. My tennis shoes slip beneath me on the salty film that covers the rocks. I taste the salt in my mouth from the wind. I get to the top of the rock first, and Pete grabs my arm to help me stand up.

Instantly I feel Erik watching Pete hold my arm. I right myself and stand a few steps back from Pete. I don't even think about it. I just do it. "What's up here?" I say.

Pete drags his arm across the horizon like he's invented the sparkling gray panorama just for us. "Ladies and gentlemen, may I present the Little Galápagos."

"The what?" says Ho-Bong.

"The Little Galápagos. That's this little island's nickname."

Ahead of us is a small patch of earth covered in huge boulders that jut up from the lake's shallow surface. The mound of gray rocks is about a mile away. Around it the lake water sparkles like a cheap bike in the March sunshine. "Do you know what's out there, campers?" Pete looks goofily happy.

"A pile o' rock," says Erik.

"No. You have to look at what's on the pile of rock. Use your binoculars."

I put up my borrowed binoculars to see the birds dotting the island. "Aren't they just gulls?"

"Not them. The black ones."

I cup my hand over the lens and look again. "Are they . . . double-crested cormorants?"

"Ding, ding, ding!" Pete grabs my hand and throws it up over my head. "We have a winner."

I drop my hand so fast I nearly drop the binoculars.

The other students crowd close to see what we're looking at. Pete yells over the wind. "They came early. What are the odds? That hasn't happened in years." He spins and drops down through the rocks, then runs for the van, I guess to get gear. Erik stands nearby, intermittently watching Pete and glaring at me.

Pritchett stands behind me and whispers, "And we have a winner."

Pete races back with his tripod and spotting scope and is set up in a split second.

"You can all look through this. I am calling my buddies

at Audubon as soon as we get home. I mean, I guess this isn't exactly a good sign. It's kind of a bad sign if birds are coming in this early. Suggests that global warming has thrown off their schedule. But maybe it's just a freak thing. You know, an irruption. Maybe . . . Maybe we should just watch them. There aren't many of them yet. I might not have even looked if it wasn't for Myra."

When it's my turn, I look through the glass scope. My eyes aren't used to the lens and it's hard for me to steady myself in the wind. Salt water stings my face and mouth. I can't make out more than black lines, and then the whole lovely bird comes into focus. One bird fills the circle of the scope. It's long, dark, and curved. Like a black S with a yellow hook on its face.

The gulls and cormorants shriek. Over the ridge of the first set of rocks I see nests made of bleached grasses and sticks. They're everywhere. So is white bird crud. Heaps of it. Boulders poke out in angry angles, rocks in the pocket of the lake. I adjust the lens for detail. Feathers and spare bones litter the ground everywhere. I see a few intact skeletons decaying on rocks. It makes the place feel haunted.

"Why do people call it Little Galápagos?" I ask. "Just because both places have cormorants?"

"That island may not look like much, but it actually has a huge significance. Birds come through here by the hundreds and nest on the island. It's too small to sustain life, but it's a perfect place to be from. Unlike the cormorants in the

Galápagos, who have lost the ability to migrate, these cormorants travel huge distances. Without this safe nesting site they'd be in huge trouble. Their numbers have already vastly decreased."

I look through Pete's scope at the nests of bleached grass everywhere. Some look old and abandoned, while others are already occupied by the slender black birds.

I say, "It's weird to me that these cormorants fly from Belize to Canada, but the birds in the Galápagos don't even leave their island."

"When you're six hundred miles out to sea, it's a much longer trip in between rest stops. The birds that tried it either didn't make it or didn't come back. The birds that stayed found what sustained them and evolved into their niche."

I'm embarrassed to be talking so much. Not my MO. But I can't help asking one more question. "Why are they here? So early?"

"Maybe they're just horny," says Pete.

I look away so he won't see my face. Everyone laughs, but Pete changes into his normal professor voice. "I mean, they are here to breed, but I don't know why they're early. Maybe the weather has them baffled. We could paddle out to them if I had my kayak today."

Dawn says, "Doesn't that bother the birds when they're nesting?"

"Great point," says Pete. "The birds come here to breed and the last thing they need is human interference. But with these cormorants, if you keep a reasonable distance, they couldn't care less about you. In that way they are a bit like their cousins in the Galápagos."

"The birds on the Galápagos really don't run off when you walk up to them?" says Pritchett.

Pete says, "Nope. Europeans killed birds and other wild-life by the shipload when they first came to the islands, but the birds still didn't develop a fear of humans."

"So in a way, the animals haven't evolved," says Erik.

"That's right. Darwin's finches, so well known for being modern examples of evolution, haven't weeded out the birds without fear, and yet they've survived. Not all the animals have survived this deficit, though. The vermilion flycatch-ers are just about gone, for example. But overall, fear doesn't seem to be steering the evolutionary ship on the Galápagos. In fact, it kind of helps to be cute and stupid because people want to save you."

"They're vulnerable as a defense mechanism?" Dawn asks.

"Doesn't play too well for humans," says Pritchett.

Erik cuts in. "I don't know. Some people know how to work it."

I'm so busy thinking about flycatchers it takes me a sec-ond to realize who Erik is talking about. I cough to keep from suffocating.

"You okay, Myra?" says Pete.

"Just thirsty," I say.

Pete pulls out his flask and hands it to me. His flask. In front of everyone.

I hold up my hand. "I'm good."

We all pile into the van again. Pete says, "Next time I bring you out here I'll bring my kayak and we'll all take turns. This is early for these cormorants. Damn early."

My phone rings. "When are you coming home?" says a whiny voice.

"Carson?"

"It's Andrew."

Andrew only has a list of about three things that make him sound like he's Carson. "What's going on?"

"Me and Brett need rides. Dad took Mel and Mom to Mel's baby class. He was supposed to be home an hour ago."

"I'm at Antelope Island. On a field trip."

"My team will forfeit if I don't show."

"I'm sorry. I don't have a way to pick you up right now."

"Thanks for nothing." He hangs up.

Everyone looks at me.

Pete says, "That's probably enough for one day."

The twins sit by each other tallying up their lists. I don't care about my bird list. I can't believe Erik thinks I'm working Pete. Of course, why else would Pete talk to me or be interested in what I have to say?

Five minutes later my phone rings again. Even in the noisy van everyone can hear it ring. I answer it. Andrew says, "How long till you get here?"

"An hour."

"The coach will kick me off the team."

I say, "I'll tell him it's my fault."

The click of the phone tells me he thinks it is.

Ho-Bong and Ho-Jun look up from their bird lists but don't say anything in English or Korean.

Dawn sits up front with Pete this time, which is fine by me. She yawns and rubs her hands in front of the heater. "So what's it like in the Galápagos? Rainy and hot all the time?"

I perch forward in my seat.

"It doesn't actually rain all that much. Mostly it mists, depending on the island and time of year. It does get hot. Sweaty hot."

"It looks so green. Is it like heaven?" she says.

He shakes his head. "When Europeans first discovered the Galápagos, they actually thought they had discovered hell. They said the land was useless. And in fairness to the Spanish, most of the islands are barren lava heaps. Only one of the islands has enough water year-round to support human life, and it's pretty inconvenient to get to the mainland. The first real settlement was a prison, but it was too hard to make crops grow and keep people from killing each other."

Dawn looks perturbed. "If it's such a horrible place, why does everyone want to go there?"

Pete drives for a few miles without responding. He has that look my dad gets when you talk about engines. "Millions of years of isolation created a place so unique that even stupid humans were smart enough to stop before we totally wrecked it. Once we did that, it kind of became this pristine jewel of evolution."

"The jewels of Isabela," I say.

Pritchett leans forward now too. "Lots of places have their

own stuff, though, right? Lemurs and Komodo dragons and crap like that. I mean, the world's full of stuff you can only find in one place."

"The world is full of many things, Pritchett, but not rareness. And the Galápagos Islands have almost a hundred and forty land and sea species and over a hundred and eighty plants that you can't find anywhere else. Per inch they're bursting with rareness."

Pritchett says, "That's like saying that if I had a wart on my face that was different from anyone else's wart that I'd like warts."

"But what if no one had ever had a wart anything like yours and never will again?"

"Still a wart," says Pritchett.

I notice that Pete is driving faster. "There is other amazing stuff about the Galápagos besides the stats for endemic species. You know that girl in the picture? She's from there. When she was pint-size, she entertained herself by riding the backs of sea turtles. Where else are you going to do that?"

Pritchett says, "I bet you can't do it there now, either."

Pete weaves along the causeway and then merges recklessly into regular traffic. "You can sit on the beach and listen to the marine iguanas snort water through their noses like little pipe organs and then follow them into the water and hear them scrape the algae off the rocks with their teeth. On one island the iguanas turn red around Christmastime and then fade out in the summer. No one knows why. There are six volcanoes on Isabela, and they go off all the time. And on Española, the oldest island, they have the only waved albatross rookery in the world. The gray chicks wander around with their parents until they get old enough, and then they drag themselves to the edge of a big cliff with a blowhole and throw themselves off, only to return home years later to mate. The whole island is crawling with red- and blue-footed boobies, frigate birds, and even Galápagos hawks. Paradise. Latitude zero."

I look up at the traffic light. "Red light," I say.

Pete hits the brakes and we all lurch forward just as he comes to the intersection. A minivan blows past us. "Wow," he says. "Thanks, Myra."

"Dude. Learn how to drive," says Erik. His is tone is light, but when I turn to look at him I see he's clenched up like a well-tanned fist. He doesn't handle surprises very well.

"Seriously," says Dawn, shaking her head at Pete. I don't think Dawn's a real fear fan either.

"Totally sorry. Don't get me going about the Galápagos," says Pete, laughing. "Once you've been there, every place else is just every place else."

When I get home I sit in the driveway. I put my head down and close my eyes. Unlike the other morning I see something besides my house and family now. I see Pete's islands. Latitude zero. I see turquoise water. I whisper to myself, "I'm going."

# 22

# Flush:

*When you scare up a bird so*
*it'll give away its position.*

I go to the library during lunch so I can surf the Web for my
project. Not like the school library has anything but junk, but
there's a computer and it's quiet. Everything is holding still so
dust can grow. I have my own little screen with a view of the
parking lot.

"Man, you're serious."

I look up from the screen. It's Erik. His square shoulders
hang over me. He's mildly sunburned, so his eyes look more
blue than they really are. "What do you want?" I say.

"Just came to work. It's quiet."

"Yes, it is," I say. I used to think he was reading my mind
with the way we would think the same thing at the same time.
Now having him this close makes me feel like I'm having a
body scan.

He rubs his hand on the desktop. "Man, it's dusty in here."

What guy notices dust? Erik.

He says, "How's your project?" His voice is quick and friendly.

"Fine," I say.

"I wish mine was. I can't even decide on a topic." He sits down next to me, like it's no big deal. "I'm sucking at this."

"Really?" This would be a whole lot easier to take if I hadn't spent the last nineteen months making out with this guy.

"It's like, who cares? How am I supposed to know what to say about stuff a million scientists have already written about?"

"It's just a proposal," I say.

"Are you still writing about those weird brown birds? What are they called?"

Erik doesn't forget facts that easily, even facts he doesn't like. "Cormorants," I say.

"I am so screwed." He puts his head in his arms on the desk. "My dad is going to kill me if I blow this off. But I can't stay up all night studying when I have work and track. And the coach is breathing down my neck as it is."

I hold still in my chair. *Don't be a doormat, Myra.*

"That sucks." Seriously, his dad *is* horrible. We hardly ever went to Erik's house to hang out, and when we did, it was to get something and leave. His mom and dad would stand in their kitchen with salt shakers that matched their granite countertops and ask us questions like a parole board.

"I swear, if the coach tells me one more time, 'This is your year,' I'm going to puke. How's it supposed to be my year when I've got a jacked-up ankle?"

"What did you do to your ankle?"

He props his head up and shakes it dismissively. "Flag football. Eddie fell on me. Can you believe that? After everything? The whole track team is pissed at me."

He's worked his butt off for that team for three years. "Wow, I'm sorry."

"Yeah. It happens." He puts his head back down.

Except I don't know what is actually happening.

"Erik," I say. "How come you're talking to me?"

"Oh." He lifts his head again and really looks at me. I can smell spearmint gum on his breath. "Shouldn't I be talking to you?"

"It's just that you haven't. Not really. Since we broke up."

He looks around the cubicle like he's suddenly lost something. He looks back at me and then starts inspecting his hands. "I was trying to be . . . straight with you, you know."

"Straight?"

"Myra. You know I miss you. Man, are you kidding? But . . ."

"You what me?"

He grimaces. "I miss you." He rubs his flush cheeks with his hand. "We were . . ."

*Come on, Myra.* "Yeah, but we aren't now."

He sighs. "Yeah." He gives me one of his perfect smiles, except now it's perfectly sad.

"Hey, I'm going to clear out of here and stop bugging you. Thanks for talking to me. Good luck with the birds. You're amazing with that kind of stuff."

He passes his hand over mine. His touch moves up my arm and goes through the circuits of my heart before my brain even knows what's happened. And then he walks out, dragging my traitorous, beaten-down, good-for-absolutely-nothing heart behind him.

# 23

# Instinct:
*Doing something without thinking about it first.*

*HE MISSES ME?*

I break at least five traffic laws driving to the marina, but I don't kill anyone or get a ticket. The radio plays a ridiculous song that Erik and I used to sing at the tops of our lungs. *Follow your heart / it knows the way back to me / this is home . . .* blah, blah, blah. I'm not sure why we thought the station was playing it for us. Probably the same reason I think that hearing it right now is karma's way of kicking me when I'm down. Or maybe it's the universe's way of telling me Erik really wants to get back together with me, but he doesn't know how. And if I would just be patient . . . and follow my heart back to him. . . . Or maybe the universe and this radio station have better things to do than worry about my love life. There's always that remote possibility.

And the problem with following my heart is that I don't think it could find its way out of a paper bag right now.

The office is a sty. Papers everywhere, a coffee cup half full, a newspaper, and a sweatshirt that looks like it hasn't been washed since you-know-who bought it from the Salvation Army clearance sale. My first attempts at cleaning were polite. Superficial sorting. Today I'm putting on the latex gloves.

Except for answering a few useless phone calls, I work like I'm possessed. Erik misses me? I need to get a few shelves arranged before I can be reasonable. By the time I finish with this dump, I'll be too tired to care.

By three-thirty I'm well beyond the desk and entryway. I'm into the hard-core cleaning of the building at large, and I feel like Lewis and Clark in virgin territory. The coffee table in the clubhouse is a different color brown when I finish. I find a dinner roll molding into a new life-form behind a reading chair. The air reeks of bleach, but at least it doesn't smell like rot. And with each square foot clean, I feel a little more organized on the inside.

An hour later, I look out the window at the marina. The sun is setting. Nearly closing time. The orange light spreads across the water as it drops behind the Promontory Mountains. I look out at the parking lot to make sure that people are leaving. There are two hatchbacks and an older SUV. Pete should be here soon to kick people out.

One of the groups is in the restroom. Two thick-necked guys in their forties. The owners of the SUV is my guess, since neither of them look like he would fit in the smaller cars. One has a dog, which he is yanking on for some reason. I step closer to get a better look. He's jerking around a faded brown pit bull. The dog's scrambling to get away, so the man keeps yanking on the leash. I can hear him yelling at the dog through the glass. I stand transfixed as the man doubles his fist and hits the dog right in the side of the head. The dog crumples then rebounds to its feet. The man punches the dog again. The dog flops to the ground. "Stay!" yells the man.

I'm out the door and in the man's face before it happens again. "Stop that!" I say.

The man is a foot taller than I am and about four hundred pounds heavier. His dog is flat on the ground, growling. At me, for all I know. The man's friend hoots with laughter, but the man doesn't say anything. We just stand there looking at each other. That's when it dawns on me that he could hit me too.

His arms are huge. He's got a ring on his finger that could break a safe. "You work here, honey?"

"Stop hitting your dog."

"You know what kind of dog this is?"

The dog's ear is bleeding down its neck. "I don't care if it's a saber-toothed tiger. Stop punching him."

"Or what?"

I lock my knees so I don't fall over. "I'll write down your license plate number and get your sorry ass arrested for animal cruelty."

The friend explodes with laughter. "You better mind her, Kyle, she's liable to kick your sorry ass herself."

The man looks at me. "Damn tree hugger."

"That's not a tree on the end of your leash," says Pete, stepping into the lamplight outside the restroom holding a wrench. He's wearing his office jacket, so he doesn't look quite as scrawny. And he doesn't look even the slightest bit afraid of the two guys. "That animal is bleeding on my sidewalk. You two better take off. It's closing time."

The two men walk their beaten dog to the SUV. The dog hops into the back obediently. I stand, watching them go, furious. That dog doesn't stand a chance. My legs start to shake. I want to grab Pete's wrench and go after both of them. See how they like bleeding on the sidewalk.

"Myra," says Pete. His voice is hard. "What were you thinking?"

"They'll kill the dog. You shouldn't have let them go," I say.

"You must come from a rougher high school than I thought."

I watch the SUV drive away, trying to see the plate, but it's too far away. Then I realize Pete is still talking to me.

". . . trust you to keep from getting killed. This lake brings out the crazies. A woman set her girlfriend on fire a block from here last winter."

I say, "I don't feel so good."

Pete scowls and puts his arm around me. He smells like grass clippings. We walk into the office. He stands in the middle of the room, looking from side to side. "What did you *do*?"

I look at my afternoon's work. "You don't like it?"

"You've sterilized the whole office."

"I'm not done, actually. I didn't file anything."

Pete steps away and looks me over. "You've got real issues, don't you?"

I sit down on the hard plastic chair. My head is fluttery. "I need to eat."

"Look at this place! I'll buy you whatever you want. Consider it a hiring bonus."

"Caffeine and french fries."

"I know just the place. But you better sit there for a minute. You look a little pale."

My cell phone rings. I look at it for few a rings and then answer.

"Myra," says Mom. "Are you on your way home yet?"

"No," I say.

"What's wrong?" Her voice is anxious. Big surprise. "Are you okay?"

"I'm just tired."

She sighs. "Okay. I need you to go get the boys. They're still over at Harper's. I just finished dinner and I'm going to be late for work."

"You made dinner tonight?" I can't focus.

"Don't be sarcastic. I'm trying to help you. You told me you'd get the boys."

We didn't have that conversation, but I don't argue. "Fine. I'll leave right now."

When I get off the phone, Pete is turning off the lights. "So no caffeine and fries then?"

"My brothers need a ride."

"Doesn't anyone else in your family drive?"

I write down my hours on the time sheet Bobbie gave me.

Pete says, "I don't get it. You just stood up to the Godzilla brothers in the parking lot, but you roll over like a shelter puppy for your family."

"I'm not a puppy," I say as I get my purse. "I'm a doormat."

"Why are you a doormat?"

I like Pete, but I don't want to talk to him anymore. I want to go get my brothers and then go to the basement and sit in the cool darkness and try to figure out what happened to me today. "Thanks for showing up, Pete. That whole thing out there was just stupid."

"Doing the right thing usually is," says Pete. "How about I follow you in my van until you pick up your brothers?"

"What for?"

"No reason."

"You think they'd follow me?"

"No. But I'd hate to lose someone who can clean like this."

"Good to know I'm useful."

"You're useful. A little lacking in self-preservation instincts, but you're useful."

# 24

# Feather Picking:
## *When a bird pulls out its feathers because it feels miserable.*

Melyssa glares at me over her toast. "Could you please stop chewing so loud?"

"I'm not chewing," I say. "You are." I mark my place in my biology book with a sticky note.

"Well, why is it so loud in here?"

Somebody got up on the wrong side of her stomach. I say, "Are you okay?"

"Do I look okay? I feel like I swallowed a microwave."

Mom isn't in the room, or Mel would get up and do jumping jacks to prove how fine she is. If Mom smells a cramp, Mel will have to go back to bed.

"What's going on?" I say.

"I can't take this anymore."

"Which part?"

"The part where my brain drowns in boredom. The part

where I can't even wear my shoes, I'm so huge. It's like being in jail from the inside. I want my body back!"

"I'm sorry," I say. "That sucks."

Mel throws her toast on the plate and it skids off onto the table. I put it back on her plate, but I don't wipe up the crumbs. That would be obnoxious.

She says, "How are you doing on your proposal thing?"

I scan the entry to the kitchen to make sure no one is listening in. "Turns out I don't know jack squat about writing a science proposal."

"Why didn't you say so?"

"Say what?"

"I promise not to actually write it. If you will please, PLEASE, let me help you do something that doesn't involve shopping for a baby, learning about babies, babysitting, or having someone probe my fat swollen bod."

I consider this for a minute. This is my project. I want to do it myself. But Melyssa does look demented with boredom, and she's a genius at making people give her money. At least she used to be.

"No writing. It has to be mine."

Her face squeezes into a smile. "No writing. I promise."

We head for my old bedroom and close the door. Melyssa revs up her laptop while I unload my backpack onto the floor.

Mel says, "The first thing we need to do is come up with a thesis so you can stop carrying around the library on your back."

"I'm writing on cormorants."

"That's not a thesis, it's a topic."

"I'm not in seventh grade. Are you going to lecture me?"

"Are you going to listen?"

I hand her my outline for the proposal. "This is what I've done so far."

She reads slowly and talks to herself. Melyssa is an audible thinker. If she really gets going, she sounds like Mr. Magoo. When she finishes she says, "This is a mess."

I start putting my books back in my backpack.

She laughs. "Relax. It's not an irreversible mess. But you're trying to cover too much. You can't write about everything that has to do with these birds. You need a niche."

In spite of how badly I hate having her criticize me, I know she's right. "Everything on the Galápagos is about niches."

"Yeah. And you're going to need something that you can really research. If you're planning on winning this thing, which you sure should."

"I thought you said my proposal is a mess."

"God didn't make the world in a day."

"Yeah, but I don't have four and a half billion years."

"You won't need it. You just need a project that you can actually research successfully, that is geared to your strengths, and that will appeal to your audience."

"Is that all?"

"Who is your audience, by the way?"

"I don't know. Some foundation." I give her the sheet that Pete handed out the first day.

She mumbles like Mr. Magoo again while she reads over the paper. Then she fiddles on her computer for a minute. I go back to reading.

In a few minutes she says, "Does he look familiar?" She turns the computer around. There is a trim, gray-haired man in a business suit facing me.

"I think he was in the slide show Pete showed us. How did you figure that out?"

"I looked up the foundation that's donating to the university. It's here on the second signature sheet in the little tiny print that says you can't sue anybody if you don't win or you fall off the boat or something."

I look at the sheet. "You mean 'the Rocky Mountain Science Institute of Biodiversity and Sustainability' gave you that guy? He looks Wall Street."

"His name is Kenneth Whitehead. He's the CEO of the institute. He's also the guy who wrote that book *God Power!*"

"The guy funding the scholarship is a creationist?"

"No. He's a businessman. A very rich businessman. Don't you ever pick up a newspaper? His book was on the bestseller list for about a decade."

"I'm in high school. I don't read the bestseller list."

"Fine. He made piles of cash selling his business management book and now he goes around promoting this idea that God wants to make you rich. He's all about getting the

Christian work ethic back in the schools and workplace."

"Why would a God-in-the-schools guy want to fund a foundation that studies the Galápagos Islands? That doesn't make sense."

"No, it doesn't. And you might want to look into that before you write your proposal."

She takes back the laptop. "He grew up around here. Well, in the city. Says in his bio that he did his undergrad at the university while working night shifts at UPS, then got into Stanford for his PhD in business. So he's no dummy. His company teaches businesses how to use the golden rule to make filthy lucre."

"I thought Jesus was poor."

"Maybe he was doing his internship. I think God has mansions of gold."

"But why would Mr. Whitehead fund this program?"

"Maybe it's that 'local boy makes good' thing. Wants to help other kids going to crappy schools."

"But the foundation is called Biodiversity and Sustainability. That doesn't sound much like *God Power!* Or making money, for that matter."

"Let's look at your assignment sheet," says Mel.

We both read over every printed piece of paper Pete has given me.

"I've got nothin'," says Mel. "This looks legit. Straightforward undergrad field research. The only weird thing about it is that they're offering the spots to Westside kids."

"Oh, who cares? What does this dumb guy have to do with cormorants?"

"Welcome to the wonderful world of getting money to go to school. You have to know how to sell yourself."

"Can't I just sell the proposal?"

"Okay, Pollyanna. You read about birds. I'm going to read about Mr. Moneybags."

In a few minutes she pushes away her laptop and lies back on her bed.

"You getting sick?"

"No. Maybe," she says.

"Thanks for helping me with this."

"I haven't helped you yet."

I look at her on the bed and I still can't believe the mound on top of her is a baby, partly because nobody ever talks about it.

"How come you don't want to know what flavor this kid is?"

"I like surprises."

"Well, he or she ought to be perfect for you then."

She tips her head up. "Maybe I don't want to get attached to it."

It takes a minute for me to get my breath back. "Are you thinking about giving your baby up?"

"I think you need to ask that guy who's advising you, Pete, to tell you about Mr. Moneybags. Ask if there's an angle on this. If you need to sound like a Christian, you're going to have to work on one of those fairy tales you're so good at with the boys."

"Mom and Dad will freak." I want to say that I'll freak, but that seems too judgmental.

"The bit you have about the cormorants' wings is good. It's specific."

"Mel, I'm serious. Have you told them you're thinking of giving it up?"

She tries a few positions to get comfortable on the bed but fails. "It's not Mom and Dad's call."

I sit with my legs crossed and keep my mouth shut.

She looks at me again. Her face is hard but calm. "Seriously. Who wants me for a mom? I'm about as mature as Carson, and a whole lot meaner."

"Yeah," I say.

"Yeah?"

"No," I say. The idea that Mel could give up her baby has never occurred to me. That's what fourteen-year-olds do. Nearly twenty is middle age for getting pregnant around this town. But Melyssa *is* mean and immature sometimes. She can also be tough and wonderful. Like how she's helping me with my paper right now. And how she didn't even get mad when I asked to borrow her car. "I'm just thinking about how weird it would be for someone else to have your baby. Like, they'll adopt it and then it would start doing math and writing poetry and being sarcastic, just like you, and you won't be there."

"I know," she says.

"Have you thought of asking Mom and Dad to take it?"

"I know Mom's planning on it, but she's not as young as she thinks."

I nod. This is way out of my league. "What does Zeke think?"

"It's not Zeke's problem," she says. "He's off doing whatever he wants."

"That must be hard," I say.

"Oh, who cares? It just means I can make up my own mind."

She hands back my outline and my assignment sheets, then drops over on the bed. Her tiny arms and legs curl around her big stomach. It seems like all that's left of her is baby. "I'd rather be writing a proposal to go to the Galápagos Islands for the summer," she says.

I tuck the papers back in my backpack. "Yeah."

# 25

# Crepuscular:
*The kind of animals that hunt at dawn or dusk,*
*like some birds and rats.*

I'm scrubbing the tables on the marina patio today with Pete's
help. It's a little early for a picnic, but Ranger Bobbie and I
agreed it looks bad when people come to the office and see
last November's ketchup on the tabletops. Bobbie also agreed
that Pete would love to help me.

"So how do you know Mr. Whitehead?" I say.

"Who?" says Pete, turning to me.

"Mr. Whitehead. You showed us a picture of him in your
slide show."

"Yeah. I did, didn't I?" He frowns and rubs his chin. I can't
tell if he's bothered by the question or by having to clean.
"He's an old family friend."

"Really? He doesn't seem like your type."

"He isn't. Why?"

"I want to research my audience."

"He isn't your audience. A panel of professors will select the proposals."

"Why do college professors care about proposals from high school kids?"

"They get paid to. Two of the profs come on the trip."

"But why does Mr. Whitehead care enough to pay them? Isn't he like a God-in-six-days kind of guy?"

"You're writing to scientists." Pete's not just bothered, he's mad.

"But it seems like it's important that we're writing for a group of people funded by the author of *God Power!*"

"Look . . . Mr. Whitehead is a deep pocket. He doesn't tell the scientists what to think. Any of them."

Pete goes out to the parking lot without another word. I go back to work inside. I have filing to do. There's a lot of junk to throw out, but some of the stuff seems pretty confidential and important, stuff you maybe shouldn't let just any high school student handle. But then again this place isn't exactly the CIA.

At five o'clock I don't see Pete. I call his cell to make sure it's all right if I leave. I get no answer. I tidy up the desk. I vacuum. No Pete. No Bobbie. I don't have any keys to lock up, so I wait. Mom will have been gone for an hour by time I get home. I know the boys are going to lose it if I don't get out of here soon and start dinner.

At five-twenty the phone rings. Technically we're closed.

I say into the receiver, "Great Salt Lake State Marina. How may I help you?"

"Yes. Yes. Is this the marina?"

"Yes." I get that about every fifth call, but people aren't usually so desperate sounding about it. "How may I help you?"

"We're still out on—" The sound cuts out, then I hear a lot of wind.

"Are you out on the lake?" I say. It's nearly dark outside and cold as all get out. I haven't seen anyone coming or going since I got here. Too windy. I look out the window. It's really windy.

His voice comes back. "Our boat capsized . . . duck hunting. 911 was busy!"

*How can 911 be busy?* "Are you in the water?" I ask.

"Yes . . . no. We got to a reef, but we're taking on water. I had this number for emergencies. We're freezing."

I get that last part loud and clear.

"We'll get someone out to you. Don't hang up. I'm calling search and rescue on my other line."

I put the receiver down and use my cell phone to dial Pete again.

"Hello, Myra," he says. His voice is rough.

"There're some duck hunters out on the lake. They're stuck on a reef. I've got them on the phone."

"Where's Bobbie?"

"How should I know? Nobody tells me anything."

"Shit. Find out where they are."

I pick up the other phone. "Are you there?"

I hear the wind in the phone. "Yeah. Yeah. The waves are

coming up." His friend yells something angry in the background.

In my other ear Pete yells, "Keep them on the line!"

"This is real bad," says the man.

The man's voice is higher, more agitated now. I slow down my voice, like I'm talking to one of my brothers when he's coming unglued. "Okay. Help is coming. What's your name?"

"Dan Anderson. My friend's Roger Wood."

"Dan Anderson and Roger Wood." I realize I need to repeat everything to shuttle information to Pete without breaking contact with the hunters. "Do you know where you are, Mr. Anderson?"

"On the lake, damn it! Freezing to death."

"But do you have anything by you that would help us find you? A GPS on the phone maybe?"

Pete talks in my other ear. "Good, Myra."

"How the hell do I do that?"

"Don't worry. It's fine. What are you by?"

"I can see the smokestack in Landon."

"Where are you to the smokestack? What direction?"

"North."

"Straight north? Do you have any islands by you?"

"The reef is out in the middle. But I think we're closest to the marina."

Pete says, "I'm going to hang up, Myra. But I'll be there in five and should be out to them pretty quick if they have lights. Make sure they have lights on. Two off-site teams will be right behind me. Make 'em hold on."

I say, "Mr. Anderson, if you have lights, you need to put them on. There are three search-and-rescue teams on their way."

"How long?"

"A few minutes. But they're coming."

We go back and forth like this for twenty minutes. During this time I can see from my office that Pete is speeding out to Antelope Island. I keep telling Mr. Anderson that help is on the way, and he keeps telling me he's freezing to death. We talk about his kids, his wife, and his job. He tells me how the waves are getting higher and he can't feel his fingers or feet. His friend Roger yells at him a few times, which is good I guess.

"Keep moving," I say. "Jump around as much as you can."

"I'd like to kick those rescue guys. Where the hell are they?"

"Close. Really close. Look for lights. Have your friend yell more."

Both men call out. The sound makes my heart sink to my shoes. What if I'm lying to them? What if Pete can't find them in the dark? What if I have to listen to them stop talking? But I don't believe I'm lying, so I guess I'm not.

My cell phone rings. It's my house. I shut off the call. They call back two more times.

"You need to get that?" says Mr. Anderson, talking to me again.

"No one I'd rather talk to than you, Mr. Anderson."

"I appreciate that," he says. "You have a nice voice." There's a long pause. "You tell my family I love them."

"You'll have to tell them yourself," I say.

"What if I can't?"

It sounds like he's not talking to me when he says this, but I answer him anyway. "You can. Hang on tight, Mr. Anderson. Help's on its way."

The phone is quiet again except for the wind. I know they are going to make it though. I just know it. It is as real to me as if they were already in.

"Mr. Anderson? Dan? You're going to make it."

Nothing but waves and wind.

Then shouting. Lots of it. Roger and Dan are yelling their heads off.

"Are they there, Dan?"

"Here! Here!" the voices explode. Then the phone goes dead.

I stand in the tidy office. I've been standing in the same position for forty minutes. Outside the wind tips the rows of masts to the water. The shingles rattle on the roof. I realize I'm sweating.

My cell phone rings. It's Pete. "We got 'em."

"Are they okay?"

"They will be," he says. His voice is flat, efficient. "You did good."

The next morning my family is watching the men being rescued on the news. I saw the Life Flight helicopter and the police arrive, but the paramedics got the two men loaded so fast I never actually saw the man I talked to.

The reporter is talking to Ranger Bobbie. "We got a distress call after closing. Normally these calls go to 911, but they had an unusually high incidence of calls last night with the storm. Luckily, our spunky little secretary, Myra Morgan, picked it up. These gentlemen are lucky to be alive. Not hard to freeze to death on this lake, especially when the sun goes down. Not a good day to go out. Things change so fast, you have to get the weather report for the whole day. Good thing they had a cell phone. Good thing they called. This story could have had a much different ending."

The reporter narrates a little background information as they show family photos of the two men, each happy and relaxed with their wives and kids around them. They look like nice guys. I wonder if they'll go duck hunting again anytime soon.

The film cuts back to the reporter standing on the marina pier. "The men were transported to the university hospital and are said to be recovering well."

The anchorwoman says, "Good thing that spunky little secretary answered the phone." She chuckles.

"Yes, it is," says the reporter.

I get a sick feeling in my stomach.

Carson talks with a mouth full of cereal. "Those are the guys you saved?"

"I didn't save them," I say. I'm a seventeen-year-old receptionist, after all.

"You answered the phone," says Andrew.

"Yeah, but I didn't get them off the lake."

"So what?" says Melyssa. "Having someone talk you through makes all the difference."

"She's right," says Dad. "That was a good thing you did. You have a way of calming people down."

"It's true," says Andrew. "When I broke Brett's collarbone, you totally cheered him up until we got him to the hospital."

Brett says, "And when I pushed Andrew out of the back of the truck and his tooth got busted, you got him to stop screaming like a little girl." The two of them exchange looks.

Dad says, "Why did I have you two again?"

The phone rings. Instinctively, pathetically, I wonder if it's Erik. Dad answers. "Yes, she is. May I ask who is calling?" He gets a serious look on his face and hands it to me. "Watch yourself," he says.

I can't believe Erik's calling me just because I got on the news. I pick up the phone.

"Miss Morgan, this is Donald Smith from KXQ. Could we interview you about your part in the rescue of the two hunters?" His voice rattles in my brain a second before it makes any sense.

"All I did was talk to them on the phone."

"We've been interviewing the men about their experiences. Mr. Anderson says you saved his life. Says you talked him out of giving up."

"He wasn't going to give up," I say.

"Didn't you think they were going to die?"

"I never thought that."

"Why not? They were in pretty bad shape."

"It's when people stop complaining that you know it's bad."

"Is that part of your rescue training?"

"I don't have any training. I'm just the receptionist," I say. I hope that doesn't get anybody in trouble, but it's the scary truth.

"You're a high school student, is that correct?"

Just then Danny comes running through the living room being chased by a tomahawk-wielding Carson. I try to cover the phone with my hand. Dad runs out of the kitchen and grabs the boys and tries unsuccessfully to make them be quiet.

"Sorry about that," I say.

"So it's kind of an instinctual thing for you then?"

"I guess."

Danny yells again and Dad drags him off to the bathroom. Carson sits down and stares at me.

The reporter laughs. "Hey, I've got younger brothers myself. That's pretty good crisis training."

There's a crash in the bathroom.

"I never know what's going to happen, that's for sure," I say.

"Thanks for your time, Ms. Morgan."


Just as I'm falling asleep, my phone beeps. It's a text from Erik.

**U r amazing! & spunky.**

I'm not sleepy anymore.

Two minutes later my phone rings. I stare at the number. The green light of my phone fills my sleeping bag. I let it ring until it stops. Five minutes later, after I've congratulated myself on my self-discipline, it rings again. I could just turn it off. I pick up.

Erik's tenor voice comes through the phone. "There are two spots, you know."

"Two spots for what?"

"We could work on this proposal thing together, if you want. I know how to write papers and you know about birds and the islands."

"How does Ariel feel about us working together?" Saying that, straight out, makes me feel almost tough.

There's a pause. "Ariel and I aren't going out anymore."

"Oh," I say. I don't ask why. I'm not a space-sucker. Plus, I don't want to hear about her.

"So, what about it?" he says. "We could just bounce ideas around. You know I'm a good editor. And I could make pie."

We both laugh. That's a joke we had last summer.

Erik took me to a musical. I'd never been to a real musical, something live and not performed by students, but I didn't tell Erik that. We went to a small theater in the arty part of downtown. On the street everyone was dressed up, going to dinner, clubs, and other shows.

We saw *Sweeney Todd*. Which should have put me over the edge, with all the blood and gore and shoving body parts into pies. But it was so smart and wicked and different from anything I'd ever experienced, I couldn't help but love it. Erik held my hand and laughed out loud and made me feel like we both belonged there as much as anyone else. Afterward he would always make pie jokes no one would get but me.

He says, "So how about it? We'll be the LHS Galápagos team."

I try to listen to my instincts, but inside this sleeping bag I can't tell which way is up. Giving each other feedback on our projects doesn't have to be a romantic thing. We could just work together. We used to be good at that. "I guess so," I say.

"Great," he says. "I'll call you."

*Great*, I think. Maybe.

# 26

# Seee:

*The finch's alarm call when a hawk shows up.*

I sit in the kitchen typing on my sister's laptop. I've had less than four hours of sleep. I feel confused about what to say next in my paper, but I keep writing because it keeps me from thinking about why I'm not sleeping. I've written three pages I can stand to keep. Scientists agree that cormorants lost their larger wings because they slowed them down under water, but I want to write about why it happened to them and not to all the other seabirds on the Galápagos. What made the difference?

What's funny to me is that the more confusing my life gets, the clearer my idea for this proposal becomes.

Mom walks into the kitchen. She came in from cleaning after one, so I know she's tired. She shudders under her robe while she makes coffee. Melyssa's right. She isn't as young as she used to be.

"What are you doing up?" I say.

"Couldn't sleep. You?"

"Couldn't sleep."

She sits down with the mug steaming in front of her face. "Dad says you're famous. You saved people on the lake."

"He's lying."

Mom smiles. "Your dad never lies."

I don't say anything, but I'd like to. The smell of coffee fills up the space between us.

She says, "You're sure working hard in school these days. Mel hardly went to class her last semester of high school."

"Yeah, well, she already had her scholarship."

Her smile disappears in the steam of the coffee. "For all the good it did her." She sighs and clinks a spoon around in her cup. "Would have been better off to send her to beauty school. At least she'd have a degree by now. You can make a lot of money doing hair."

"But Melyssa wouldn't be happy."

"She's not too happy now. I hope you'll be smarter."

"I'm working on it."

"You're working on something." She leans her head into Melyssa's laptop.

I sit still and let her look. I know it won't mean anything to her. Nothing about what I'm doing with my life makes sense to her. "Just a science paper."

She leans back and looks me over. I do the same to her. Having Melyssa home is wearing us both out. She says, "I want you to be happy, Myra. But being smart isn't going to bring that boy back to you. He's a spoiled rich kid, and you aren't. You're just too different."

We sit in silence.

She says, "False hope can kill a person. Part of being happy is knowing where you belong."

"I know, Mom."

"Not yet," she says. "But you will." She takes her coffee and goes back to her room. Her steps sound like sandpaper on the cold linoleum floor.

# 27

# Stoop:
## *To dive hard and fast.*

The first day of school after the hunters got pulled out, a few teachers ask me about the rescue. Mostly kids don't watch the news, so it's no big deal. But by the second day, everyone and their cousin has heard about it.

Jonathon sits by me in bio. "So how does it feel to be a spunky little celebrity?"

"I wouldn't know," I say quietly.

"What do you mean? You're a star. I've watched the clip ten times myself. Crappy footage. Should have given you a full-on interview. Missed the real angle. So typical of podunk local coverage."

"Do you want to share with the class, Jon?" says Ms. Miller.

"Myra's a rescue ranger."

Ms. Miller raises her eyebrows at me again like she did the day I told her I was going to apply. "Really?" Apparently Ms.

Miller is the only one in the city of Landon who hasn't heard.

"She was on the news. She's like a rescue worker at the marina now and she talked these stupid hunters off the lake when they were going to give up and freeze to death."

"They weren't stupid," I say. Why does everyone think you have to be drunk or stupid to get stuck on the lake?

"You're the girl who did that?" says Ms. Miller.

I hate how surprised she looks. Again.

"Do you want to tell us about it?" says Ms. Miller.

Erik turns to look at me and smiles. Tight T-shirt girl stares. The weird thing is I always kind of thought it would be fun to be like Melyssa and Erik and be the center of attention. Turns out it's embarrassing.

"It wasn't a big deal," I say.

"Yes, it was," says Jonathon.

Ms. Miller says, "Jonathon, stop talking and give that girl some peace."

When I get in the car to go to work, I turn my phone on and see I have a text from Erik.

> Come over after track? Parents in Phoenix.
> We can use both computers.

I click off the message and feel the heat in my face. I remember what happened last time I went to Erik's house when his parents were out of town. It didn't involve the computers.

None of this matters, of course, because after work I have to go home and get dinner on, clean up, and help the boys with their homework and do my own, which has been all the way off my radar since I started spending every spare minute reading about birds and islands in the middle of jack nowhere. Plus I'd have to lie to go, because Dad would freak if I casually mentioned I was going to visit the kid he now refers to as "the little puke."

I turn on Melyssa's stereo. Of course *the* song is playing. Is it me, or do they just play that song every ten minutes? It doesn't matter. The stupid lyrics crawl inside me and before I know it I'm thinking about how it was to have Erik talk to me in the low, happy way he saved for when we were all alone. Then I'm thinking about how it felt to have his arms around me. How he sometimes smelled like citrus. What he sounded like when he started breathing too hard, which is kind of like wind on a loose screen door, and my stomach started doing a quadruple twisting layout, and I'm just really grateful I'm nearly to the marina because I shouldn't be driving when I'm out of my mind.

Ranger Bobbie is in her office for a change. When I walk in the door I can smell her ice cream. It must have something in it besides mocha and almonds.

"That was a great thing you did with those hunters." She digs into her quart with a spoon.

"Thanks. I feel weird about it."

"Why?"

"Because what if I had screwed up?"

"You didn't. Shake it off." Bobbie looks annoyed. I'm ruining her ice-cream break.

"The kids at school keep talking about it."

"Let 'em talk. They didn't save anybody's life this week. You're way too hard on yourself. That's supposed to be my job. Anyway, how about rescuing a few dirty windows this afternoon?"

"Love to," I say.

"Good girl," says Bobbie. "You bring your worries to me anytime. I'll find you something to clean."

Bobbie and I have what Ms. Miller calls a mutualistic relationship.

The sun feels good on my back. I can't stop thinking about whether I should go over to Erik's. Before I know it, I'm scrubbing the glass off the windows. I decide to block out Erik by thinking about how much money I need to earn before I can apply for the Galápagos. The next thing I notice is that my ladder's moving. "Hey!" I yell.

I look down and see Pete rattling the back legs. "Don't you fly? I heard you were Super Office Girl."

"Hey, I'm going to fall if you do that."

Pete rattles the ladder harder. He's laughing but I'm not. The last time I saw him, he was fuming at me about the whole Mr. Whitehead thing. But even if he's ticked, this is taking it too far. I drop my towel and grab on to the ladder with the hand that isn't holding the window cleaner. The momentum sways the back of the cheap aluminum legs and I careen off into the air.

I fall smack into Pete's arms. He's surprisingly strong for a skinny guy, but I'm bony too. My knee hits him right in the mouth, which is fine with me, except it hurts my knee. "What are you doing?"

"Hey, do you want to go sailing? The wind's perfect today." He doesn't even put me down first. I mean, I nailed him and he just holds me there, grinning.

Just then Bobbie comes whipping around the corner and sees me in distressed-damsel pose. I slide out of Pete's arms. Pete rubs his mouth. "You made me bleed, Myra."

"Myra has work to do," says Bobbie. "And so do you. In my office."

I see Pete leave the office a few minutes later and he's not exactly smiling. I stay outside, doing windows where it's safe. By the time I finish, the afternoon is gone and I have a sunburn on my arms.

I slip inside quietly to finish up. Bobbie nabs me as I wipe down the counters. "Pete's just a big kid. That's why we like him around here. But you're a real kid. You get my meaning?"

"Yeah," I say. My face suddenly matches my arms.

"I like you," she says. "I'd like to keep you around, okay?"

"Okay."

She grabs a set of keys off the wall. I notice she's put her firearm on. "Got a couple of drunks trespassing over at the Saltair Pavilion. Hate that place. See you tomorrow."

The Saltair Pavilion is a rebuilt version of a dance hall that should never have been built in the first place. It's burned to the ground three times, but nobody seems to get any smarter.

I walk out to the garbage containers with the trash and watch Ranger Bobbie drive away. I wonder what it would be like to be so fearless. A woman who chases off vagrants without flinching. Not to mention that she pays her own bills and buys liquored-up ice cream she has no intention of sharing. Now that's spunky. I bet she'd never call Erik or go over to his house just to see what would happen. I bet she never does anything that people want her to, unless she wants to.

I run into Pete at the storage sheds. He's cleaning off a gang tag that's been there awhile.

"Did you get in trouble with Bobbie?" I say.

"What did she say to you?" he says.

"She told me I'm a kid."

He keeps scrubbing. He's a good scrubber for being such a slob.

"I'll see you tomorrow," I say.

"Hey, no. There was a reason I knocked you off the ladder."

"There was?"

"Yeah. You have a minute?"

Pete stows his cleaning gear in the marina golf cart and we drive down the road that drops into Sunset Beach. The sun isn't setting yet, but the water is lit up and sparkling. We take off our shoes and walk on the coarse white sand. The water has left deep furrows in the ground, lined with brine shells and tiny white feathers, almost like a planted crop of birds. The sky is lit up and endlessly blue.

"I got mad the other day," he says. "And I'm still kind of mad."

Pete's face looks as sunny as the sky. "Really?" I say.

"My dad's kind of a sore spot with me."

"Your dad?"

"Actually my whole family . . . We aren't close. Not like you and your family."

"You've lost me," I say.

Pete digs his long foot in the sand. "Daniel Whitehead's my father. Mr. God Power himself."

"Seriously?" I guess I should have figured this out, but they don't exactly look alike.

"I left home when I was sixteen. When I found my way back here to get my PhD, he set up the foundation to kind of bribe me or smoke the peace pipe or something. And I told him it was fine as long as he kept his religious views out of it and the foundation funded kids going into research who didn't have a lot of family backing. The only hitch was his raise-a-thousand-dollars thing, because he's very into self-sufficiency, unless of course you're talking about his own kids, whom he buys sports cars and Ivy League college degrees and chubby Latin maids who make great guacamole. Not that I'm bitter."

"Not at all," I say. We walk a ways more in the sand while

I try to refigure everything I know about Pete. "So you're rich? And that's why you're mad at me? Or at him?"

"Right."

We are nearly into the water. There's a fringe of brine shrimp exoskeletons that gives the lake's edge a cool, seedy vibe. A fishy smell fills the air, even though there are no fish in this water. Gulls wail overhead. Pete picks up a rock and skips it a long way out.

"Where did you go when you were sixteen?" I ask.

"I was a basic runaway. I hung out around the local viaducts with all the other homeless kids at first. Then I hitched to South America."

"Shut up. How did you get the nerve to do it?" I say. "How did you get across the border?"

"Fake passport. I wouldn't recommend it."

"Yeah, I'll keep that in mind." My head spins with questions. "How did you get a different last name?"

"I changed it."

"You changed your name to Pete Tree?"

"I like it better than Peter Whitehead. Anyway, I don't want to talk about it. Mostly I was a mess for a long time. What I want to tell you is that you can write what you want to for your essay. The judges don't care who you are, or what religion you aren't. They want a person who will chase an idea. Someone who can take risks and believe in themselves."

My eyes drop to my watch. "I'm so late."

"I'll take you back."

"Thanks for telling me about your dad. I won't say anything to anyone."

"I know you won't. You're kind of an old soul, Myra. You get it."

"I'm not sure I do, Pete. Why is your dad in the picture in class? Did he come visit you down in the Galápagos?"

"Yeah. He's writing another book. It's about how nature proves that there's a God or some other really unique idea. He came down and took a lot of people to lunch for a month. Including the girl in the picture."

"Your girlfriend?"

Pete makes a whistling sound through his teeth. "Not anymore."

We bump along in the golf cart toward the marina office. "He chased your girlfriend off?"

"It was kind of a father-son project."

"So you can work together, I guess."

"Listen. We don't get along. But at least this project will help somebody."

Pete walks me to my car and opens the door. I say, "Why do you think I have an old soul?"

Just for a minute Pete looks serious. "You care about people, and you're a little tortured by it. How old are you, anyway?"

"Eighteen," I say. "In May."

"What day?" he asks. I like that he doesn't make fun of me.

"May first."

"May Day! That fits you. What are you going to do to celebrate? Feed orphans or solve global warming?"

I punch him in the arm and he acts hurt.

"I don't know what I'll do." The thought of my birthday really depresses me. "Not go to my Senior Dinner Dance. It's that night." It's so sad that I know that. I guess I'm not such an old soul after all.

"You're a knockout. You must have a million guys who want to take you."

I get inside my car fast. My face is bright red and it's not because I'm sunburned. I don't want to talk about my love life with Pete. "I'm damaged goods at my school. But it's fine. It's almost over."

"Does this have anything to do with that Erik kid? The one who's always giving you the stink eye?"

"He does?" I say.

"If no one else asks you, I'll take you," says Pete. "As a friend."

I don't know what to say. It's ridiculous. He's five years older than I am. And I don't even care about going. Or at least I wish I didn't care. "You can't. You're my teacher or whatever."

"Teachers give grades. I'm a cheerleader."

"You're my boss. Sort of."

Pete laughs and leans in the window. "You can just say no, you don't have to make excuses. Dang, I must be losing my touch."

"It's just . . . Aren't there some rules about this?"

"You worry way too much about rules." Pete has a talent for being sweet and rude at the same time.

"Fine." I have a talent for liking guys who get me into trouble. It's probably a really bad idea. Who cares? "Let's go."

"But only if someone else doesn't ask you, okay? I don't want to break up any great high school romance you have brewing."

"Don't worry." I turn on my engine.

"That's the great thing about me," says Pete. "I don't worry."

"That is the great thing about you, Pete. Thanks."

# 28

## Suet:

*Bird food made out of boiled beef fat. Yum.*

When I get home the boys are playing basketball in the drive-way—except Danny, who has somehow turned the hose on and is trying to flood the basement through the front yard.

"Didn't you guys see that he had the water on?"

Even Carson looks bored by my question. "He wasn't hurting anything."

I stare at my sidekick. Carson's grown in the last month. He's playing basketball instead of digging up dinosaurs. The older boys aren't making fun of him. What is going on around here?

"Where's Mom?" I say.

The three boys shrug their shoulders and keep playing.

When I go inside I hear Mom's shower. That means she's running late. The kitchen and front room look like we've been ransacked by the mob. I step through the crime scene and put a full gallon of milk back in the fridge.

I peek in Melyssa's room. She's asleep with her mouth open. She'll be up all night watching TV.

I tap on Mom's door. "Can I help?"

Her voice calls back. "How about coming home on time for a change?"

I think of me on the beach with Pete. "Sorry. Things went late."

"Now *I'm* late."

My cell phone vibrates.

Erik: **Can u come over tonite?**
Me: **What for?**
Erik: **New Galápagos movie.**
Me: **Maybe.**

His words flash back on my phone, as quick as his smile.

Erik: **I'll call after run.**

I tell myself it doesn't mean anything. He's got a movie about cormorants. We're friends.

By the time Mom flies out the door, I have three colors of leftovers put together in a bag for her dinner. I hand off the paper pouch and she hands off the chaos. We're a team. Not a good team, but still a team. I follow her out into the driveway to make sure she doesn't run anyone over as she pulls out going fifty. She waves as she disappears down the empty street.

Danny runs to me. Even his eyeballs are muddy, but they're wide enough that I can tell there's something wrong. "I can't make it stop," he yells.

I follow him around the house. Before I see it, I hear the thud on the back window. By the time I get there, the bird is lying on the cement patio with its neck bent.

I point at Danny. "Don't touch it. It was sick. That's why it was flying into the glass."

"Is it dead?"

I get down a little closer and look at the bird's sealed eyes. "Yeah. You go play. Without the water on this time."

I get the shovel from the garage quick, before the boys have time to make a party of the little thing. It's not the first time a bird has plowed into this window, but usually they get the idea after the first collision that they should fly in the other direction. Some birds are slow learners. I lift the bird onto the shovel and then put it on some newspaper and take it to the trash. The sound of it dropping down to the bottom of the bin is about as lonesome a sound as there is.

Out of sheer guilt for all the things I'm not telling my parents, I make my dad's favorite dinner. Meat loaf. No kidding. The guy goes crazy for the stuff. To me it's a brick of hamburger with ketchup. But after two servings Dad leans back in his chair and says, "Simple pleasures. Makes life worthwhile."

For some reason this depresses the daylights out of me.

Dad says, "You better get Melyssa up if she's going to make it to her pregnancy class with Zeke tonight."

"She's going with Zeke to her class?"

How am I missing all these things around here? Last time I heard they weren't even speaking.

"Her doctor recommended it."

"Has the doctor ever seen Zeke and Mel in the same room?"

Dad pulls out a toothpick and pokes at his teeth. "Now. Come on, sweetie. Sometimes all a good man needs is a second chance."

"When did you decide that Zeke was good?"

"I don't know if he is or not. But not everyone is born good like you, Myra. Some people need to grow into it."

My one-track brain does another lap about Erik and tonight. Why does my dad always say the absolute wrong thing at the right time?

By eight thirty the boys are winding down for the night. Erik hasn't called. I don't know if I'm more irritated with him or myself. I walk into Andrew's room, where he and Brett are reading.

Andrew drops his novel on the bed. "Your pirate story is better than this one."

Brett looks up from his comic book.

Carson peeks his head in the door with Danny right behind him.

"Well, where were we then?" I find myself surrounded by four boys before I drop to the floor. I have no idea why my brothers humor me the way they do.

Carson says, "The people from the town had to learn to talk to the birds to go. That's what you said."

"Yes, yes, our friends had to learn to speak Gruntn-screech."

"What birds speak that?" says Brett.

"Good question. Birds have as many languages as we do, but there are certain things they have in common. These were seabirds. And like pirates and other sea creatures, their language involved a lot of gruntin', swaggerin', and squinty-eyed cursin'."

"And singing. All pirates sing," says Carson.

"There were just five townies left, trying their luck for the hazardous honor. So the pirate king took them all onto the ship for a final test of sea legs and savvy. 'The sea be a watery desert where a soul can die o' thirst or hunger, less'n he learn to hear what the birds be tellin'.'"

Danny starts sucking his thumb.

I put my hands to the side of my chin like a sweet and saucy scullery maid. "'But how do ye know, Cap'n Pirate?'

"'Ye have to think like one,' says the pirate king.

"So the would-be pirates parked themselves on board and traveled down the coast in search of talking birds. Not far down the rocky shore the wind stopped. The clouds came in and the crew got bored. So they did what pirates always do when they get bored. They got stinkin' drunk. Except the maid, on account of her prim and proper stomach. Instead she watched the birds and wondered what it would be like to fly over crests of water for days, riding the wild wind. In her mind she saw the world of sky and water. Then, as the maid was standing on deck having such deep an' salty thoughts, she heard the cry of a gull, and then another. They were swirling on the horizon around an outcropping of rock. *Why*, she wondered, and soon got her answer. A boat so small it was nearly impossible to see in the waves. She raised the alarm. The pirate king looked into his telescope and whistled. 'They be wavin' for help, boys. Their ship be sinkin'. Hoist the sails!'"

"Do they save them?" says Danny.

"As they pulled forward toward the dinghy, the gulls began to scatter. The maid searched the sky and water. She saw bread floating in the waves. *Why would drowning men feed the birds?* she thought. She listened to the birds' thin calls. And what she heard was fear. 'Look again, Cap'n,' she called in haste. 'It's a trap!' The pirate king laughed but humored the maid, only to see from behind the rocky outcropping another pirate ship emerge. Yet thanks to the savvy scullery maid there was still a chance. The pirates fired their cannons and sent the bad boat smoking. The other ship's pirates tried to board, but the pirate king and his crew were ready. And the new recruits showed themselves as fierce as any other mates. Soon throats were cut. Sad but true: pirate blood floated on the salty sea."

"Awesome," says Andrew.

"Arrrr, 'twas awesome awful," I say. "But thanks to the savvy maid, alert to birds and bandits, the good pirates and their guests weren't hacked to briny bits. And the lousy, no-good pirate ship was sunk to the bottom of the cold sea. Now that the test was done, the brave crew returned to the town of Deadendia to make their last preparations for a voyage to Isabela."

"So who gets to go?" said Brett. "Besides the dumb girl."

"Aye, the scullery maid had read the signs of the birds to save the day. But the others were brave. Plus, later that day, three crew members ate the town meat loaf and came down with landlubber disease. So all five of the townies set sail for Isabela to retrieve the magical jewel."

I stand up and hold out my hands. "Time for bed."

"That was okay," said Andrew.

"Whatever," says Brett.

Maybe Dad was right about the pleasure thing after all. I send the boys to bed and turn off my messageless phone. I'm surprisingly calm about being blown off. I have homework to do. Good homework. Not Erik-in-a-dark-family-room-homework. Much later that night I fall asleep with my mind stuffed with facts and pictures of birds from all over the world. When I dream, I am surrounded by wings.

# 29

# Home Range:
*Where specific birds hang out,
not their whole species.*

When I see Erik the next morning I don't say hello. In fact I
don't say hello to anyone, because I've got a homework hang-
over. The upside is that I know things I didn't know yesterday morning, like that birds have two voice boxes, and some
can sing a duet with themselves. Some birds migrate sixty
thousand–plus miles in a year. Half the birds that fly south for
the winter never come back. Birds are intense.

So is getting up at five a.m. on a Saturday after two hours
of sleep.

"Hey, how are you?" says Erik. He stands next to me with
his arm against the wall.

"Hmm . . . ?" I step away from the wall.

"Sorry I didn't call last night. I ran the Skyline loop and
my ankle hurt so bad when I got home I just fell asleep."

I say, "Don't worry about it." I have an underdeveloped

vocabulary for telling Erik to get lost, even when I think he's lying to me.

"Something wrong?" he says.

"Why would anything be wrong?" My voice is three-fourths whine and one-fourth sarcasm. It's going to take some practice to get the mix right.

Erik smiles his pointy white smile. "No reason. But your shirt's inside out."

Pete yells through rolled paper. "All aboard!"

I climb into the back of the van and sit next to Dawn. She looks like she's had a night even longer than I have, except her clothes are on right-side out. "What's up?" I say.

She ignores me.

Pete bellows again, this time from the front of the van. "Everybody ready for an adventure?"

Pritchett climbs in next to Dawn and looks us both over. "You two go to the same coven last night?"

"Shut your hole," says Dawn.

"Yeah, I like my women spicy," says Pritchett.

Dawn says, "How do you feel about fatal? You like your women that way, Stretch?"

I comfort myself with the knowledge that if these two kill each other, there will be less competition for the scholarship.

We head out to the freeway, but today we turn back toward Landon.

"Where are we going?" says Erik.

"In the Galápagos Islands you have to be aware of the

relationship between things. So today we're studying geology while we look at birds and mammals. We're going to Yellow Rock Canyon."

"Where?" says Ho-Bong.

"We're going clear to the copper mine?" says Erik. "Geez, can you get me back for graduation?"

"We'll get you home in time for lunch. Anybody else who's going to turn into a pumpkin if we're gone a few hours?"

"Why are we going to the copper mine to study how to write a proposal for the Galápagos Islands?" asks Ho-Bong.

"At least three of you in this van aren't going to the Galápagos Islands, so I thought I'd teach you something about your local habitat."

"That's cheerful," says Dawn.

"The first thing I want you to do is look out the window. By the time I get to the entrance of the canyon, I want all of you to have a one-sentence description of the town you live in. Everybody got paper?"

"What's the point of that?" says Erik. "Is that part of our application?"

"A good scientist understands his or her tools. And you're a tool, Erik."

Pritchett and Dawn burst out laughing. Okay, I laugh too, but quietly. The twins look at Pete like Erik has a point.

I say, "You want us to think at this time of the morning?"

"Discovery doesn't happen when it's convenient," says Pete.

I look out the window as we pass the mobile home park along the freeway. I see the towers on the roof of my high school that make it look like a juvy center. Main Street looks like a mothballed movie set. All around Landon, urban sprawl is creeping to the corners, but in Landon, life plugs along, stubbornly unchanging, except to keep becoming more and more outdated. And yet it's a town where everybody knows who you are. You can't fall down in the street without getting a hand up. There are four seasons. I live near mountains and deserts and lakes. They just aren't places I go very often. I live in my house, car, classes, and job.

When we get to the trailhead for Yellow Rock Canyon, Pete asks for our sentences.

"My town is a soulless suburban wasteland," says Dawn.

Erik reads his. "Landon is a town of hardworking people who care about their community."

"We live next to a park that has a pond with floating cans," says Ho-Bong.

Ho-Jun says, "There are three grocery stores within two miles of my family's store."

"How about you, Pritchett?" says Pete. "What's it like living in Graniteville?"

"It's like living on the funny farm," he says, "except no one laughs."

The group turns to me.

"I live between an industrial rock and a suburban hard place."

"Nice," says Pete. "And now for something completely different."

Yellow Rock Canyon begins at a craggy trailhead with a half dozen signs telling people that they can't drive their four-wheelers in the area. There are tracks right under the signs. Farther up the trail the trees are starting to leaf in and grass is sprouting from jaundiced yellow to muddy green. Cotton-woods and willows line the stream that cuts down the canyon. Overhead Pete points out the turkey vultures. "They always fly in twos."

"Why?" says Ho-Jun.

"They pee on themselves and throw up in their nests to keep away predators. They sort of have to stick together to have company."

Dawn says, "Sounds like my stepbrothers."

Pritchett says, "What else you got besides vultures, Pete?"

Pete nods. "You name it. Bears, cougars, hawks, elk, deer, eagles . . . and in a few months this place will be like a singles bar for migratory birds."

We walk farther up the soft trail and come into a brushy meadow. A jackrabbit bolts in front of Dawn and everyone says, "Ooh." Except Dawn, who trips into the mud and swears a blue streak.

"They really do have huge ears. I thought people made that up," says Pritchett.

Pete shushes us. "Listen."

The air floats with gobbling. Pete points to a stand of trees, and a huge dark shape waddles into view. "Wild turkey, male, looking for company."

The giant bird makes a sound like, "Ke ke. Putt putt." His brilliant blue head and red wattle twist with irritation. He doesn't look real, he's so bright and blue.

"Should I give him my number?" says Dawn.

"You aren't his type," says Pete. "But the mud is a nice touch."

The bird flies up a few feet and lands. He seems more disgusted with us than frightened.

Pete puts out his arms to shush us again. The bird watches us and then begins making a strange, low, throbbing sound. Definitely X-rated.

"Strumming." Pete uses his low, throbbing voice. "Maybe you *are* his type, Dawn."

Right on cue, three females flutter over a hill and prance around in plain sight. Pritchett quietly laughs. "This dude is popular."

The birds ignore us and bob their blue heads. The ladies flutter. The male struts.

"Shake it, Turkey Lurky," says Pritchett. Even Ho-Jun and Ho-Bong crack up.

"And Cocky Locky," I say.

"You're a bad little girl, aren't you?" says Pritchett. He puts his arm around me, and then I crack up.

"I might surprise you," I say, just because I feel like it.

"I bet Myra is full of surprises," says Dawn. She looks more cheerful covered in mud.

Pritchett laughs and keeps his arm around me.

"Is this really what we're doing today?" says Erik. "Watching birds have sex?"

"Right," says Pete. "I don't want to fill all your impressionable minds with animal behavior. Do not try this at home, children. Let's head to the van."

Pritchett drops his arm.

I look through my borrowed binoculars. "Do we have to go?"

As we walk back, four turkey vultures swoop overhead. Squirrels bicker in the trees. Four deer sprint through the scrub oak, stirring up dead leaves and branches. A bald eagle chases away the turkey vultures. The sun filters through the cottonwoods, speckling the ground. The springwater rushes in the walls of the canyon. We're thirty minutes from my house and I never knew this place existed.

When we get back to the marina, everyone heads for their cars. I go to mine to put my stuff away and regroup before I go to work. I feel Erik walking behind me, but I don't see it coming when he climbs into the passenger seat of Melyssa's clunker.

"Excuse me," I say.

"What was all that about today?"

"All what?" I say loudly. Pritchett and Dawn both look at me from their cars as they drive away.

"Why are you doing this?" Erik's face is blotchy.

"Doing what?"

"Do you really want to go to the Galápagos Islands? Really?"

Hearing Erik say this out loud makes the idea seem ridiculous. "Why do you care?"

"Because I think we need to talk." He looks at his hands.

"About what?"

"About us."

My pathetic space-sucking heart is hammering. "What us?"

He puts his hands down at his sides, balling them up and then extending them. "I wanted to talk to you last night. But the truth is I didn't have the nerve. Not after everything that's happened."

"Talk about what?"

"About us. I miss *us*. I miss you."

"There isn't an *us* anymore," I whisper.

"Couldn't there be?"

Just like that he says it. The question stares me in the face. But it doesn't look like I expected it would. The idea feels more ridiculous than trying to win the scholarship.

He says, "Do you have to go to work right now? Let's go for a walk."

I look around me at the marina, trying to get my bearings. I *do* have a few minutes before I have to be at work. I watch the wind carrying small sailboats out to the center of the lake. I think for a split second about my dad saying that sometimes you need to give a good man a second chance.

"Where do you want to go?" I say.

There is no smile now. He says, "You can follow me in your car. I'll surprise you."

We're all alone in the parking lot. This is my call. I watch him get into his white truck. I turn on my radio. That stupid song is playing.

What do my instincts tell me to do?

All I can hear is the song.

I follow him.

# 30

# Swooping:
*When birds attack.*

We don't drive far. Erik speeds up the frontage road that goes back behind Saltair. There are a few Saturday cyclists on the road, but mostly it's deserted. He pulls over and motions for me to come get in his truck.

I walk up to his window. "What are we doing?"

"Hop in."

The music from the song in my car gets quieter in my head. Instead I hear the whistle of the trains coming across the desert. The sound has to travel a long way to reach me, and yet somehow it does. "Not to be rude, Erik, but the last time you had a surprise for me, it wasn't a good one."

"Well, I can't break up with you again, can I?" He laughs.

"I've got to go to work." I turn to get back in my car.

Erik hops out. "Hey, don't be mad. I'm sorry. That wasn't funny. Let's just walk for a minute." He takes my hand. His grip surprises me.

The road dead-ends in a trailhead a ways from where we've parked. The birds are going crazy with the warm weather. A little gray finch dive-bombs us from a lonely oak tree. It's a rosy finch, but I can't tell if it's black- or gray-crowned because it's moving too fast. Its sharp body makes me step back, which cracks Erik up. In the willows, red-winged and yellow-headed blackbirds are tweeting their lungs out. Overhead the gulls are circling. A great blue heron floats a thermal over the marshy shore. A raft of American coots bobs below, keeping tight so eagles won't pick them off. A slender crane tips back and forth, pumping the water for food. Two months ago I might have noticed these birds, but not like I see them now. Now they are bright and loud with names and histories.

"Look." I point to a northern harrier hawk sunning on a post. Its feathers gleam gold and brown in the sun.

"You're really into this bird thing."

I shrug. "Birds go places."

Erik nods and keeps on walking. He looks exactly like he did the day he broke up with me. His black hair is jutting in all directions. He moves gracefully through the tall grass. When he turns to look at me, his eyes are lit up with a light I don't understand. It's not just that he's so good to look at, it's that there is something about him that draws me in, like vapor to glass.

"What did you want to talk about?" I say. We are a long way from the road.

"You get right to business these days. That's cool."

I wait.

He rubs his mouth and he laughs. "It's just hard to put it out there, you know?" He puts his hand on my arm. My heart starts sprinting again. I want to listen, but I don't. What if he wants to be with me? What if he doesn't? Why am I afraid?

The irritated finch comes for us again.

Erik swats at it with his loose hand and the bird squawks louder. "That puny thing wants to kill us."

I say, "Did you know that the smaller a bird is, the bigger its heart is? Hummingbirds have the biggest one. That's why they can fly so fast." I sound like a tour guide. I sound like Pete.

Erik keeps his hand on my arm and puts his other hand on my chest. I hold very still. We are off the trail, completely alone. It's not like he has a gun to my head or anything. But not all weapons are made of metal.

"Yours is going pretty fast." He picks up my hand and puts it on his chest. "Happy or scared?"

"Why should I be scared?"

He smiles. "You're always scared."

"Fear's a useful defense mechanism."

"Not if you're afraid of everything," says Erik.

*Come on, Myra.* "What did you want to talk about?"

Suddenly Erik hauls off and kisses me. And honestly, I miss being kissed, so the kissing would be fine if I didn't know what was on the other end of it. I pull away.

"Myra, come on," he says. "Just breathe." He takes my arm and pulls me forward, so now we're sitting on a dry patch of grass by a bush. He starts kissing me again. Like I'm not even there. And suddenly it's like that weekend when his parents were out of town. When things got all messed up.

And then I realize what I'm here for.

I was wearing his mom's apron. I know how that sounds, but I always cook in an apron. It's like my ironed money, I just like it better that way. He came up behind me while I was breaking the spaghetti noodles into the pot and put his long arms around me. When he held me like that it made me feel so good, like we were almost the same person. He said, "I love spending the day with you. I mean, the more I'm with you the more I want to be with you. It's like time doesn't even matter, except after a while we remember we're hungry."

We'd been hanging out in the hot tub, and we were starving. We stood there in his parents' kitchen with the swirling granite countertops and chandeliers like you see in hotels, dripping water from our swimsuits on the kitchen rug. He started humming that song from the radio in my ear in little tenor pieces. I think I could have stayed like that for the rest of the day.

But then, after a minute or two, his hands started moving. Too much. It's not like I was innocent of the whole thing. I'd been there most of the day enjoying it, until I wasn't anymore. About the time he started pulling off my suit.

I shrugged him off. "I'm cooking."

"I know."

"I don't want to, Erik." That's what I said.

He kept smiling like I was kidding. "Don't want to what?"

I moved and kept stirring the pasta. He turned off the stove. "Hey! Let's go in my room. I'll be good. Scout's honor." He held up three fingers, like he was hilarious. Like he was doing this for an audience. Or maybe he was doing it for himself, so when he was eating Sunday dinner next week with his parents he could remember that he had said that to me right in the spot where his mom makes pot roast in her tacky sunflower apron that says "April Showers Bring May Flowers."

He rubbed my shoulders. "Why are you like this, Myra? You act like you love me and then you just freeze up every time. I'm the one who's going to hell, right?"

"Nobody's going to hell. I just don't want to do it on your kitchen floor."

"I was thinking the same thing."

He took my arm and started walking to his bedroom.

The voice in my head was having a shouting match with the other voice that wasn't saying words, just noises. Noises that told me I did love Erik, and I loved being with him. And there was nothing wrong with it and it's normal and natural and blah, blah, blah.

I pulled my arm away. "I don't want to do it in your bedroom either."

"Just keep breathing, Myra. Don't be scared."

I was scared, but not like he thought. We'd been close to this before. But I was scared because I knew that this was going to make things different.

Then he kissed me again, pushing me into his room backward. And it didn't feel good. It didn't even seem like this was about me, or even Erik. It seemed like it was all about us being here and his parents being out of town so this was what we were supposed to do. It felt like a mistake.

"It'll be fine."

"I don't want to."

He pushed me hard onto his perfectly made bed, like my brothers would push me if they were kidding. But Erik wasn't kidding. He didn't even seem like Erik.

"What are you doing?" What I meant was, *What is wrong with you*? But I didn't say that.

"What do you think?" He leaned over me and pulled down the top of my suit. He was smiling, like this was a big party. But everything felt wrong. Everything. Especially me.

I put my arms up, and without meaning to, hit him in the cheek. Not hard, but he stopped. Angry. Like I'd never seen him. He wouldn't force me. But I'd humiliated him.

And then he said, "Are you too stupid to know how this works?"

Erik knows a lot of stuff I don't. He knows how to win. He knows how to be smart. He knows how to make people think he's a good guy. He knew I would pretend like this never happened to keep him. But, just for that moment, I knew enough to pull my suit back on and hang his mother's apron on his bedroom door. I knew enough to run.

The finch is still barking behind us. Erik says, "Is this about Ariel? Because she's not an issue."

"I couldn't care less about Ariel."

"What are you afraid of then?" he says.

I take back my arm. I say, "What are *you* afraid of?"

He rests his arms on each side of me. "That you and me aren't getting back together." He sounds completely sincere. Framed in sky and grass, Erik is beautiful. And horrible.

I take a deep breath. "Did you dump me because I didn't sleep with you?"

He shakes his head in disgust and moves away from me. "I just asked you to get back together with me and that's how you treat me?"

"Did you?"

"Of course, I'm the bad guy. Not that you freaked out, or that you were clingy, or that I just needed some space."

I can't believe he's saying these things to me just seconds after he asked me to get back together with him. The speed that he moves from one personality to the other, that's what I felt at his house. That's how I knew, but I didn't realize what I knew. "I think you're going to have to get someone else to work with on your proposal."

He turns to face me. "What, like I need your help? Give me a break. I'm not cleaning out my sock drawer."

I get up from the ground. I rub my mouth with the back of my dirty sleeve. I wish I could wipe off every slimy, hypocritical kiss. But more, I wish I could wipe away the memory of how much I treasured them.

I want to walk silently, stoically away. That's what I would have done before. That's not what I'm going to do now.

I take another long breath. "You're a conceited, spoiled

pretty boy." His eyes get wide and then narrow. His perfect smile is gone. "This is not a bluff. If you ever try to push me down or throw yourself at me again, I'm going to tell the entire world that you tried to jump me in your mom's apron. I mean, you so much as touch me and I'll beat the pansy shit out of you myself."

Erik says, "Nice mouth."

"Goes with the rest of me."

"Your words, not mine."

I'm not listening to his words. I'm walking back to the car as fast as I can.

He yells, "No one would believe you anyway."

I call over my shoulder, "No one but Sophie. Doesn't her mother have lunch with your mother every Tuesday?"

A few seconds pass and then I hear Erik's feet.

I'm within sight of the trailhead right when he catches up. "If you say a word to that bitch . . . She's the biggest gossip in three counties."

"Nice mouth."

He takes my hand and I shake it free. He's not going to touch me again.

I hear a honking horn and look up. Ranger Bobbie is sitting in her truck. She waves.

Erik and I walk to the road and separate without speaking. I move quickly to Bobbie's window. I don't think she's sightseeing.

"Where you been, missy?" She's wearing an empty holster. Her gun is on the seat.

"I'm sorry if I'm late."

Erik's truck passes us.

"Damn. He's driving the speed limit," she says.

"Of course he is."

She puts her gun back in the holster. "What was that all about?"

"Nothing."

"You sure?"

My knees wobble. I lean on the window of the truck and try to act like I'm just being friendly. I look into Bobbie's wrinkled, freckled, beautiful face. "I could use a ride back to my car," I say. "And maybe some of your ice cream."

"You can have a ride," says Bobbie. "But you gotta carry a permit for the ice cream."

# 31

# Striking:

*When a bird bites you to let you know
who's in charge. Not you.*

The only good part about school for the next week is that nobody expects me to do much brain crunching anymore, except Ms. Miller. The rest of my teachers are as sick of school as I am. There's the busy work that goes with the "transition" into "real life" (which doesn't sound ominous or anything), but mostly school is just about showing up now.

Unfortunately, that means I have to show up in biology with Eric. But thankfully, Jonathon is all about this movie he's making so he manages to keep me distracted.

". . . then my cousin put his hand right in the blender and I had my camera totally focused on him the whole time."

"How did his mom like you filming while her kid got maimed?"

"That was the best part. The tattoo on her forehead actually changed color. There was blood in the batter. Isn't that a great title?" He holds out his hand so I can see it in lights. "'Blood . . . in the Batter!'"

Ms. Miller sighs loudly in our direction. Her hair looks grayer than it did when we started the school year. She points to her timeline on evolution. I thought we had covered this unit, but she seems to be circling back to it for some reason. "We don't take up much room. In fact, we are hardly a blip. But we've changed the way the earth does business. For better or worse we have altered the earth's chemistry."

"If we blew everything up tomorrow, wouldn't it all eventually go back to how it was before us?" says Jonathon. "All that stuff in the timeline?"

"Time only moves in one direction, Jonathon. It's reasonable to think the earth would be less polluted without us around, but depending on what we did to exterminate ourselves, that might not matter much."

"Isn't that assuming that all this is just random?" says Erik.

"We aren't talking about the purpose of the earth, Erik. Just the history."

Jonathon studies the board for a change. "Like, I see what you're saying, Ms. M, but how do you know any of this? How do you know that evolution isn't some bogus theory. Like spontaneous generation? Or, like, how do we know that the way we figure out the age of everything isn't wrong? Maybe our whole idea of the universe is wrong and we're really just a dust speck on a giant cosmic dandelion."

We all look at Ms. Miller.

"Well, aside from the fact that we haven't found any evidence to support your 'Horton Hears a Who' Theory, there are some things we can almost know. I say 'almost' because nothing is absolute. Let's look at evolution. What did Darwin discover that made him question the popular beliefs of his time?"

I say, "One thing he saw were finches that were adapted to each of the Galápagos Islands. It didn't make sense to him that God had made each one of them from scratch."

"Nicely put, Myra. Let's make it personal. Do you see any evidence of evolution in your own family, or in your own life?"

"You mean like how my family gets taller with each generation because we marry hot, tall women?" says Jonathon. He nudges me and clucks.

Ms. Miller nods, frowning.

"Tall kids and finches with funny beaks don't necessarily mean that God doesn't exist," says Erik.

"Of course not," says Ms. Miller. "Many people, including Einstein, believe, or believed, there is a divine origin to evolution. But our understanding of evolution does suggest that a certain amount of change is inevitable and what direction that change takes can alter the future permanently."

The tight T-shirt girl says, "Well, duh. We'd all die of boredom if nothing changed."

See, there you go. Just when I thought I knew everything, I learn something in school.

The bell rings. Ms. Miller points to the reading for next time. "And I need to see Myra after class."

The class says, "Ooh . . ." in unison.

Ms. Miller waits until everyone is gone. I organize my backpack about six times until the last person walks out the door.

She sits close to me and fingers a file folder. "There's been a complaint."

"About what?"

"About your application for the scholarship."

"I haven't even turned it in yet."

"There is a concern that you're getting extra help on your application."

"From whom?"

"I can't tell you that."

"Who's helping me, or who's complaining about me?"

"Either."

We sit looking at each other. I would love to tell her the whole gory story just to make sure she felt sorry for all the times she'd ignored me and treated Erik like an academic demigod. But then I realize that Erik fooled me too. I can't expect Ms. Miller to believe me.

"Erik is mad because I'm not giving up." I'm not going to talk about the other reason Erik is mad.

She taps the folder. "These are serious complaints, Myra. Not just about you."

Okay. That rips it. I dig in my backpack and hand her my notes. "No one is doing my homework but me. Unless Pete's dictated all eight drafts of it to me."

She reads through my latest draft. She doesn't skim. The other class is filing in, but she keeps reading. Her face retracts into a giant frown. Why should she believe me? I'm Myra, the boy parasite. I don't know if she's frowning because it's bad or because it doesn't prove Pete hasn't helped me, but whatever the reason, she looks seriously depressed by my ideas on cormorants. Then her face does this melting thing. It's so much worse than the disappointed face. I wonder if she's going to cry.

"Ms. Miller?"

"All this is your work? Pete hasn't seen it?"

"No. I mean, he tries to help all of us in class. But a lot of the technical stuff goes over my head, so I don't even know what to ask. I have more work to do. I can make it better."

She shoves back my papers. She doesn't even straighten them. She looks me in the face and frowns again. She coughs. I must be in bigger trouble than I thought.

She says, "You have to look past the people who don't believe in you, Myra. Sometimes we're just too tired to notice. But that's no excuse. Neither is a phony little creep with a 4.0." She drops her fist on the folder. The kids coming into class stop talking. "Win or lose, don't you wimp out, honey. Don't you dare!"

I don't mention the complaint at work. But I stay away from Pete. Ms. Miller may be the teacher, but she doesn't know Erik like I do. He knows how to win. And now it's more than a field trip for both of us.

# 32

# Twittering:

*Short birdcalls to keep in touch with members of
the same species. Birds did it first.*

By Friday I'm seeing sea turtles and cormorants in my breakfast cereal. I hear dolphins squeaking in the dryer instead of
bathroom mats. I've dreamed of the Galápagos every night
for a week. I walk around the house in a sun hat and cutoffs.
I expect to start speaking in fluent Spanish at any moment.

Friday night I come home from work and make artifi-
cial crab enchiladas and canned mango smoothies. I get the
smoothies done before my mom leaves. She gives me this look
like I need to be in an institution for the criminally goofy. But
she licks her lips when she drinks it. "What's the occasion?
Are we all taking a cruise?"

"Why not?" I say. "You'll be staying in the deluxe cabin,
with a masseur and a cabana boy to do your bidding."

"Could he start by working my shift tonight?"

"I'll check with the captain."

Mom rolls her eyes. "How about you fill up my cooler with

another round of this stuff? Is it legal for me to drink this and drive?"

"Yes, Mother, it's virgin."

Melyssa waddles into the room and sprawls across a kitchen chair.

Mom says, "I'm glad something is."

"Nice, Mom," says Mel. "Real nice."


After dinner we are all so stuffed we have to lie on the living room floor like beached whales. Mel is the most convincing. I'm not sure how we're going to get her back up. My dad joins us, but on the couch with a newspaper. The smell of the seafood lingers in the house, heavy and sweet.

"Story time," says Carson.

I've never told any of my stories around my parents. It's a violation of the code. And I'm exhausted from cooking and eating too much. "Maybe later," I say.

"Come on."

Melyssa attempts to roll on her side and fails. "Yeah, why do you always hide in the bedroom when you tell your stories?"

"Because they're bedtime stories."

"Don't you have any I-ate-like-a-pig-and-I-can't-move stories?" she says.

"Yes, but they all have sad endings."

"Tell your pirate one," says Andrew. "That's not sad."

"It is tonight."

"Does the prince die?" says Carson.

"The prince?" says Melyssa. "We can only hope."

I lower my voice. "Where were we when last we left our pirates?"

"They had just escaped the bad pirates," says Danny.

"Indeed they had, mate. And now, with a few barrels of food and drink, they were off on the real journey. Sailing the sea for the island of Isabela."

"Isn't that the big one? That had an earthquake last year?" says Melyssa.

"It's a real island?" says Andrew.

"Yeah, it's one of the Galápagos Islands," says Melyssa. "Didn't you get that?"

"All righty then. I'll be telling this tale, missy, and I'll be thanking you to put an extra-strength sock in it."

"Sorry," says Melyssa.

"The trip was long but beautiful. The wind was with their sails. Almost as if the breath of Fate herself was driving them. The closer they got to this mysterious island, the warmer it became. Gulls, terns, and albatross—which are not actually bad luck at all—escorted them in a grand parade. The sails sang with the gentle hum of the travelers. The fish trailed in the ship's wake; they seemed so lucky in speed. The sun warmed the crew's bones in the morning and sparkled on the water in the evening. But all was not well on the magical cruise."

"It never is," says Brett.

"So true. For it seems that the prince was not keen to share the glory of his conquest with his fellow Deadendiers, especially not the mild scullery maid."

"She's so annoying," says Brett.

"Not as much as you are," says Andrew. The two scowl, but no punches are thrown.

"On the last night before they were to set anchor on the beloved Isabela, the prince had a very unroyal idea."

"Did he poison her?" says Andrew.

"No. Her nose was too keen. But he did poison the crew with lies. Lies of the darkest kind. He told the crew that she spoke the language of the birds because she was a witch."

"He's mean," says Danny.

"Arrr," I say. "Too true. The prince may not have spoken bird, but he spoke pirate. And a masterful storyteller, he was. When he was done weavin' his web, even the pirate king himself couldn't convince the simple-minded crew that the prince was lying. In fact, the prince even told them that she had gotten unfair help in passing the bird test. He claimed she had bewitched the pirate king and taken wicked advantage of his pirate heart! Called her cheater and a . . ." I look at Danny. "A wench."

Melyssa shoots me a look of disbelief. Sometimes it's nice that she gets me. "He did not."

"Oh, yes, he did. In no time at all they had the poor maid on the plank, headed for her doom. And they were thinking about putting the pirate king up next if he complained. So off she went."

"You have got to be kidding me," says Mel. "I'm going to kick the tuna out of that kid."

"Don't worry, she's the main character. She can't die," says Brett forlornly.

I give Brett the evil eye. "And off the plank she went. Sinking to the bottom of the beautiful blue sea. Sinking. Sinking. Sinking . . . in a cold, salty tomb."

Danny puts his thumb in his mouth.

"But just as she was surrendering her last innocent breath, she felt the slice of a hard object at her tied wrists and feet. It was none other than the knife of the mean old first mate, who had slipped off the ship and come to her rescue. It seems the first mate had fallen in love with her biscuits and he couldn't bear to have her die. When the maid burst through the surface, the crew thought 'twas a sign from the sea. They decided that the prince was probably exaggerating the whole witch thing anyway since they'd had such an easy trip getting there."

"Did they make the prince walk the plank?" says Andrew.

"No. He was a royal, even if he was a royal pain, so they decided his punishment would be that everyone would treat him like a peasant from then on."

"That's not good enough," says Mel. "They shoulda killed 'im. With their bare hands."

"They were landing on the island of Isabela and they had bigger fish to fry."

"What happens next?" says Carson.

"My little brothers go to bed is what happens next."

"Awww," says Danny. "I wanna know if they get killed by natives."

My dad lowers his paper. "Me too. I love a good killing by the natives." I had no idea he was listening.

"There'll be plenty of time for killing people tomorrow," I say. "Bedtime."

"I think the prince gets knifed by an angry native and turned into soup," says Melyssa.

"No." I sigh heavily. "This is a realistic fairy tale."

# 33

# Thermals:
*Rising warm air, perfect for bird joyrides.*

It's our last day of class. As I drive to the marina, I look longingly at the sky, streaked with yellow and rose. Summer's coming. I roll my windows down, even though it's cold. Noisy robins line the old trees on the side of the road. The smell of grass and flowers comes in waves.

Pete is standing in the office talking on the phone when I come in. "It is a lot of money. I agree," he says.

I go into the club room and see Pritchett and the twins. No Erik or Dawn. Ho-Bong and Ho-Jun look like they're on their last supercylinder. Ho-Jun's hair is actually messy. Come to think of it, so is mine.

Pritchett says, "Hey."

"What's up?"

"Dawn's out," he says. "She's on the phone with Pete right now."

I feel sick. "Why?"

"Hard to make a thousand bucks selling lattes."

"I know about that," I say.

"Not me," says Pritchett. "I have a good gig."

"What do you do?"

"In a band."

This shouldn't surprise me. Pritchett reeks of personality. I just have never met anyone who's really in a band. "No way. What do you play?"

"Bass, vocals, and style."

"Huh. Are you any good?"

"Good enough to make more than I would selling lattes."

Pete walks in. He's not happy. "Okay. We're going to make it short today. Dawn's out of the competition and Erik isn't coming because he has a track meet. The due date for your proposals is May first. That's three weeks. When you have your work done, all you have to do is mail it in. Otherwise I can help with questions. I hope you enjoyed the tour."

"We came down here for nothing?" says Pritchett.

I have to admit I'd feel the same way, except I have to work in an hour.

"Do you have any other questions?" says Pete.

Pritchett throws his backpack on his shoulder with a dramatic sweep. "Do you think I'm going to need to get the SPF 30, or will I be okay with 15?"

"I'd hand your paper in before you pick out your Speedo," says Pete. "If there's nothing else, I have a ton of work to do."

Ho-Bong and Ho-Jun walk to Pete and hand him two envelopes. "We're done."

"That's great, guys, but I want nothing to do with your papers. Just mail them in and the judges will make their choices. I am not a judge, juror, or referee for any of it."

"Well, I guess that's it then," says Pritchett. "Nice knowing ya."

I'm sorry to see the last class end on such a sour note. I know Pete's mad about Dawn, and I suspect he's heard about Erik's complaint.

I say, "Hey, Pete? Do you have one last cheer for us, before we go?"

Pete scowls. "I would need caffeine and seven more hours of sleep for that this morning, Myra. But you go for it."

I pull out my chair and climb up on it. The four guys in the room look up at me like I've sprouted wings. I think about my chicken moves and start it up.

"When I say 'go,' you say 'south.'"

"Go."

"South."

Pritchett's the only one who chants back when I point to him.

"Go."

"South," chants Pritchett.

"When I say 'Galápagos,' you say 'Islands.'"

"Galápagos."

"Islands."

"Galápagos."

"Islands."

"When I say 'gimme,' you say 'money.'"

"Gimme."

"Money."

"Gimme."

"Money."

"Goin' south to the Galápagos 'cause I'm so stinkin' funny. With all your stinkin' money. Go Galápagos!"

I finish with the traditional jumping jack in the air and a graceless thud to the ground. The crowd (Pritchett) goes wild.

I work a boring shift for most of the day. The weather is so nice I wander around outside looking for a reason to be out on the pier. I show tourists the best place to wade in the water. I take a few pictures for families. There's a little excitement when a couple gets their boat stuck in the channel and no other boats can get out. I call a few people to help and get yelled at by frustrated boaters, and eventually everything goes back to boring.

Ranger Bobbie comes in off the desert at lunchtime. "Four-wheelers!" she says, and slams her door. I see Pete while I'm cleaning a picnic table. He says, "Tourists!" and storms off.

When my shift is over, the sun is still high in the sky. I know I should go home and take care of my brothers while my parents finish their backyard fiasco, but I sit at the picnic table watching the birds. The gulls are everywhere, looping in the sky, diving for food. I pull out my notebook. I'm just three weeks away from reaching my goal of a thousand dollars. My pencil-box bank is getting full. Driving the smaller car and skipping lunch have helped. With any luck I'll get a few bucks for my birthday too.

I feel hands cover my face. I jump away.

"Somebody's edgy," says Pete.

"Self-preservation instincts," I say.

"Nice to know you're using them these days. You logged out yet?"

"Yep, on my way home."

"Want to take a spin on my sailboat?"

"Don't you have to work?"

"This is work. We're having a mini regatta for the yacht club tomorrow morning and some of the buoys aren't where they're supposed to be. I could use a hand."

All the weirdness of the last few days since Ms. Miller told me about Erik's complaint runs through my head. I can tell by the edge in Pete's voice that he knows what we aren't talking about. And he doesn't care. That's why Pete is Pete. He doesn't care. That's why he can go to the Galápagos Islands or hitchhike to South America.

I look out over the shimmering water. It's a gorgeous day. And I want to go sailing with a pirate.

"Sounds fun," I say.

My phone rings. It's my house. I don't pick up.


Pete shouts out the names of a dozen different ropes for me to pull and tie as we leave the dock. Who knew that sailing was so complicated? I bounce from side to side of the small boat, trying to get the hang of tacking first, which is basically moving the tail of the sail into alignment as we're "coming about" or turning into the wind. Then I work on jibing, which mainly involves throwing ropes and scampering across the front of the boat and not getting clocked by the mast. As we pick up speed, a hundred pounds of home blows off my shoulders.

We get to the buoys in twenty minutes and have the problem fixed in thirty. It was hard, but I don't think Pete needed my help at all.

"Where to now?" I say.

"We'll hoist the spinnaker if we get a little more wind, but let's just relax for a minute." We drop the anchor and Pete pulls out his pack. He tosses me a sandwich and a can of soda. "Sea rations."

I sit at the front of the boat and let the sun warm my skin. The salty wind opens my lungs up. I smell the brine and salt beneath me. "Tell me more about living down there," I say.

He lies back, eating his sandwich while he looks up at the sky. He doesn't answer for a few minutes. "In the morning when the sun comes up over Isabela Island, the sky lights up with red-streaked clouds. Sometimes there will be a gold flare coming from behind the island's dark silhouette. The gulls and sea lions circle the boat looking for food. The waves lap up on the anchored boat. Drying clothes flap in the wind. Everything smells like the ocean until someone starts to cook and the frying food reminds me I'm starving. But I don't want to go in with the team, because then the day will start, and before I know it, it will be over. The trick is to hold on to each day as long as I can, and then once it starts, I go till dark. Turns out there's a lot of daylight at the equator."

"Every day is like that?"

"Not at all. Some days it's so hot you sweat in the water, and other days it rains and the water is so rough we can't dive or eat or even drink, which is saying something."

"I keep thinking about that quote you read from Darwin's journal, about not knowing what you should be looking at until it's gone. What don't I see?"

"That's easy." He hitches up half his mouth. "How amazing you are."

I love that Pete is almost flirting with me, but once I stop being giddy, I think about what he's saying. And he's right. I look up at the same sky Pete does, but I don't see the same thing.

Pete keeps talking. "You also don't see where you are. You want to go to the Galápagos because it's not here. And you should. But there's plenty here to blow your mind if you'd stop trying to please everyone all the time."

"You sound just like my sister."

"Smart girl."

"Yeah, she's a genius. So smart she got pregnant before she married the guy and then dropped out of school and lost her scholarship."

"And that's why you're trying to please everyone?"

"I've always tried to please everyone. I'm just not very good at it anymore."

Pete rolls in the anchor. "Let's go find another place to park."

With a quick wind we curl around to Antelope Island in forty minutes. I try not to wonder what the phone call from home was about. I comfort myself by knowing that if it were a big deal, they would have called me a half dozen more times.

Pete drops anchor in Farmington Bay. He pulls out his binoculars to share, and we quickly spot mergansers, scaups, green-winged teals, canvasbacks and redheads, egrets, and grebes, all winging around, chirping and diving. It's a bird frenzy.

"Every year this lake has five million feathery visitors and two hundred species. And the lake effect . . ."

"You told us . . ." I say.

"Do you know that without this bay and the other stop-over habitats that this lake provides, the ecosystem of the earth would change?"

"Should I be taking notes or taking a nap?"

"Cut the attitude. This lake is beautiful and important. And most people think it's a sewer."

"What did you bring me out here for, Pete?"

"Most people don't want to grow and change and discover new things, Myra, not really. But you do. Be a student right now. See your life."

He sits next to me and takes my hand, looking off into the

water at the heron that is coasting on the air above us. There's no wind, but I feel like I'm sailing again, and I could pitch off into the water at any time. And I love it.

"You're beautiful and important."

"You're just saying that because I scraped the mold off your office."

"No. I was fine with the mold. It gave the office a little personality. I'm saying this because I find you beautiful and important."

I look up at his face. His hair is deep red in the sunlight. His eyes are pinched in a smile. In my head I know getting attached to Pete could cause us both a lot of problems. Plus he likes mold. But somewhere deeper than my head, I feel like Pete is nothing if not honest, and this is only wrong if I make it that way.

I hold my face up to his and he kisses me as softly as the sun.

# 34

# Sluicing:

*Shooting a bird off the water.*

Dad is sitting by the front room window. The kids are watching the TV up close so they can hear it on low volume. They all five look up but nobody talks.

I say, "What's wrong?"

They all keep looking at me. The sunshine of my afternoon empties out of me. "Where's Melyssa?"

"She's in her room," Dad says. "Don't go in. She's asleep."

Mom walks past us into the kitchen and I follow her.

She turns to me. "Where were you when we called?"

"What's going on?"

"Answer your mother's question," says Dad, sandwiching me between them.

I sit down at the table to get some breathing room. "I was out on the lake."

He sits down next to me. "On the lake? Like on a boat?"

"I was with Pete," I say. I don't feel like hiding the mess

under the rug anymore, but it's one of those moments you can't take back.

Dad's voice lowers. "Pete who?"

The amount of information I haven't shared with my parents hits me like a flying filing cabinet. "Pete Tree. He's kind of my boss but not really. . . ." I think I'll skip the part about kissing him this afternoon. . . . "We were having lunch." Too much. Always better to shut up when you don't have a grip on your story.

"Just how old is your kind-of boss?"

I say, "Can you tell me what's going on with Melyssa before we get into this?"

"No, we cannot," says Dad. He jabs the kitchen table with his finger.

Mom says, "Why don't you start by telling me what you and Melyssa are up to?"

"Up to?" I say. "She told you?" So like Melyssa.

"She didn't tell us anything. But we'd like you to start explaining right now."

"I'm sorry, what are we talking about? Did I do something?"

Mom drops into a chair too. "This is no time to hide things. Your sister got very sick this afternoon. We took her to the doctor and he said she has preeclampsia. Do you know what that is?"

I shake my head. "Is she going to be okay?"

"We think so." Mom tilts her head toward me but is looking someplace I can't see. "She has to be on bedrest until the baby's lungs get developed enough to deliver. The most important thing is that she doesn't get more toxemic. If she loses the baby she does, but we aren't losing her." Mom is so calm it terrifies me.

"How long does she need?" I say.

She says, "At least another month. Some babies get by with a lot less, but some don't."

"A month. We can do that."

"We can," says Dad, "if one of us is with her at all times, which means one of us needs to be here after school until I get home. Andrew isn't old enough to drive, so it's not safe to leave him in charge."

"Okay. That means I need to be here at four, right? I can be here by four. But I need to keep working."

Dad says, "Why? What's going on with you, Myra? What's the money really for?"

Mom goes to the loose paper file by the phone and brings back the application information that Melyssa and I were working on last night. I remember now I left the papers sitting right on her dresser. "And what do you know about this? Why is Melyssa applying to go to South America with a new baby?"

"She isn't," I say.

Mom's voice drops. "Then who is?"

"I am."

"You!" says Mom. "Really?"

"I'm applying for that scholarship to the Galápagos Islands with the University of Utah."

"The Galápa-what-the-hell Islands?" says Dad. He leans so hard on the table it jiggles under his weight.

My brain stumbles. "Ecuador. Darwin's—"

"Yeah, I know where they are, honey. What I don't get is why you think you're going there? I thought you were going to dental hygiene school."

"I told Mom about it, but she said it was a stupid idea."

"We talked about this?" says Mom.

"It's a great opportunity, but I have to raise a thousand dollars. And submit one of the two best proposals. We're down to five applicants from three schools."

"A thousand dollars? Absolutely not," says Mom.

"It's less money than the dental assisting school," I say.

"But you'll have something when you're done with school. This is a vacation."

"It's two months of serious scientific research. We work with professors and get college credit."

"Two months?" says Mom.

"Really?" says Dad. He looks so hurt I have to think of cabbage to keep from crying.

"Oh come on, Hank. Two months, an eighteen-year-old girl on a boat thousands of miles from home. Over my dead body. Even if Melyssa—"

Dad stands up from the table. "And you've been hiding this from us the whole time. Sneaking around, working on something like this without a word? What are your chances of getting it?"

This is so not the way I wanted to tell them. "I'm competing against Erik. And some other super brains. But I have a chance."

Dad's eyes get even wider. "Erik? You're trying to beat Erik out for a scholarship?"

"Don't act like it's so impossible!" I say. "Pete says I have a good idea."

"Pete! Who is Pete? I thought he was your boss at the marina."

"He's not really my boss-boss. That's Ranger Bobbie. Pete's the harbor master. He's also the graduate student who's helping us all write our proposals for the contest."

"And you're sailing around the marina having lunch with him?" says Mom. "Oh my gosh, you aren't . . . sleeping with him?"

"No, Mom, no!" I say. "I am not sleeping with him! I'm not even sleeping. I work around the clock to do my homework, make dinner, keep things clean, do my research, work, hang out with Melyssa and the boys." My eyes burst, but I'm not sad, I'm furious, at everyone, including myself and Melyssa and Pete.

"Keep your voice down, young lady," says Dad.

"You're not applying," says Mom. "Your sister needs you. And it's ridiculous."

"Do you think you can beat Erik?" says Dad.

"She isn't applying!" says Mom. "Two months on a boat in the middle of nowhere with complete strangers? Has everyone lost their minds? This isn't even about that. It's about Melyssa's life, and the baby's."

Carson walks in the room rubbing his eyes. He looks at me happily. "If Mom's yelling at Dad, does that mean we can turn the sound back up on the TV?"

We all three yell, "No!"

Carson runs out of the room.

"So what is it going to be?" says Mom. "Your vacation or your sister?"

"Oh, Marci, don't exaggerate," says Dad. "We can find someone to do it."

"And just who would that be?" says Mom.

*Who would it be?*

The question wraps around me. My parents both work themselves to death as it is, and neither one exactly calms Melyssa down. Someone has to pick up the kids from school. Someone older than eleven has to be around between four and five-thirty. And a paid nurse? Forget it. Too much money and too many Morgans. I hate Mom for sounding that siren inside of me, but once I hear it I can't pretend I don't. Sometimes you just need someone calm to calm you down. Someone you trust. And that can make all the difference.

Later that night, I peek into Melyssa's bedroom. She's hunched up in a ball snoring from a cold. I think of the birds and the turtles and the sun. I think of what it would be like, for the first time in my life, to be on a crew that isn't a cleaning crew.

To study something interesting and real, and hang out with people who are from all over the world. I would finally have something that belongs to me, a future. And win or lose, competing in this contest is a victory for me, against Erik, against Doormat Barbie. Then I think about Melyssa. How she lent me her car and her laptop, dared me to apply, and made me mad enough to follow through. In her own seriously irritating way, she has helped me through this breakup with Erik like no one else could. And she's my sister.

I have a choice.

I choose her.

# 35

# Winged:

*When a bird's been shot but doesn't drop dead.*

"You can't quit," says Pete. "We're heading into our busy season."

"Bobbie said she can hire someone else."

My conversation with Bobbie was cut short by her having to go outside and yell at some unruly boaters. But she said she understood about family coming first.

"She lied. We can't replace you."

"Thanks, Pete." I keep my distance.

"Is this because I kissed you?" he whispers.

I can't look at him. "That's not why."

"Follow me," he says. He walks out to the picnic tables. Even with the muted sound of Bobbie chewing out the boaters on slip four, it's beyond beautiful today. The lake is glistening with the light of spring. The wind jostles the masts of the docked boats expectantly. The group being yelled at is just another sign of spring. It won't be long before summer is here and all the owners of all these boats are crawling over them and taking them back out to open water. Pete has just mowed the lawn around the office and I can smell it everywhere. Inside the office everything is clean and in its place. Outside everything seems blue and white and possible. But it isn't.

Pete hops up on one of the tables and shakes his head. "Why are you doing this?"

"My sister needs my help."

"Can't anyone else help her but you?"

"Not this time."

"Exactly. This time. The time when you need to make money so you can leave and stop being everyone's maid."

"You like me being your maid I've noticed."

He doesn't laugh. "I don't want you to be anyone's maid, especially not mine."

"Thanks," I say. "Anyway, this should make the judging easier, though."

"You're still going to apply, right?"

"I don't have all the money."

"Apply anyway. You can make it up if you win."

"But that wouldn't be fair to Dawn and other people who dropped out because they couldn't get the money."

"Who cares? I thought you were developing your self-preservation instincts."

"I guess it just depends on what I want to preserve about myself."

Pete shakes his head. "I can't figure out if you think you're better than everyone else or worse."

"This isn't about me. It's about being part of a family."

He jumps off the table. "Like hell it is," he says. "You're chickening out. It isn't even about the trip. You just can't stand the thought that you might be happy. It would throw off the whole save-the-world thing you've got going."

I wouldn't expect Pete to understand. He cracks jokes and drives a car without windows and doesn't worry about anybody. That's fine with me. "So I guess I'll see you around then."

Pete turns away. He's watching Bobbie and the boaters. From the looks of it, the guys are giving her some grief. My last shift is over and we both have to go. He turns back to me.

"You'll see me at six o'clock sharp next Saturday, thank you very much."

"For what?"

"I believe we have a date. For your birthday. Is seven better?"

"You still want to go to the dance, even though I'm quitting?"

He says, "You think you have the corner on the martyr market?"

"I'm not a martyr."

"Yes, you are," says Pete. "And you're about to be an eighteen-year-old, pretty martyr, which is the very worst kind. Look what happened to Joan of Arc. Not good."

"At least she died famous."

"Famous for being dead is still dead."

"That's not what she was famous for." I do a fast-forward, imagining Pete showing up at my senior dinner dance with a beard and his harbor master clothes. I put my hands together in a Joan position. "See you at seven."

# 36

## Rehabber:
*A person who is supposed to know what
to do with messed-up birds.*

I've threatened the kids with broccoli for dinner if they're late
for me to pick them up at the curb from school. Actually,
Carson likes broccoli. But there's no more lollygagging. We
are all on a schedule now. Four days down, twenty-six to go.

When I get home, I immediately go hang out with Mel
and tell her about my day while she lies there on her side like
a pinned animal. I brought her some books from the library
about pregnancy. But she can't really read because it's hard to
hold a book in that position. So I've read some to her and then
read a lot more to myself. Turns out preeclampsia is kind of
interesting.

One day I paint her toenails green. One day we search her
laptop for pictures of fat celebrities and she actually laughs for
about ten seconds.

A lot of the time we just sit in the same room. I know she's
mad I'm not applying for the scholarship, but we don't talk

about it. Usually by the time Mom leaves, Melyssa goes back to merciful sleep and I start dinner.

Today when I come in she's watching a soap. Her hair is matted to her head in a lovely roadkill updo. Her skin is ashy and swollen. The room smells like cheese puffs and apple juice. She ignores me. I override my urge to power wash the room and instead sit down next to Melyssa and her idiot box. A makeup-caked bimbo is about to get her clothes torn off by a guy who could be her father. I watch the woman throw herself at the rich old creep. What is it with women and older men? Such a cliché.

"Those shows will kill your brain cells," I say.

"So will being a mom," she says.

"Exactly. You might want to hold on to a few IQ points."

She puts another wad of cheese puffs in her mouth.

I stand up and start cleaning. I can tolerate the stench of junk food but not her self-pity.

Mom has made up another bed in the room so she can sleep next to Melyssa during the time I'm at school. Which I think is hilarious, because Mom sleeps so hard after she's been working all night that Mel would have to fall on her to wake her up. Beside Mom's folded blankets there are home improvement magazines. And a basket of unpaired socks. I can't get away from those lonely socks.

"Sorry, I'm a grouch," says Melyssa. "Crappy day."

"What happened?"

"Nothing." She wriggles her feet up onto her pillow at the base of the bed.

"You talk to Zeke lately?"

"Zeke who?" she says. "He's probably out writing some deeply pathetic poetry about how dark his life is. Either that or out getting drunk."

"Since when is Zeke a drunk? Isn't he in school?"

"I don't know where he is." Melyssa gets up on her elbows with a heavy sigh and turns off the TV. "I called his phone yesterday and the number was disconnected. So I called the house and the shrew who runs the place said he'd moved out. No forwarding address. Too bad, that was a great house."

"You have no idea where he is?"

"I did suggest he go to hell. I guess he could be there."

"I'm serious. He's your baby's dad. What if something . . ."

"He's *not* a dad. He's a self-absorbed sperm donor. Like this is going to ruin his shot at writing the great American novel or something. I hope I never see him again."

I look at Melyssa's puffy face. Her shadowed eyes flutter around the room, taking inventory. I don't know what she sees, but I'm guessing it's four walls and nothing she wants.

"And you are a worse liar than I am," I say.

"I'm not lying. He's gone."

"That doesn't mean you don't care."

"Fabulous. What good does caring do?" says Melyssa.

I stack Mom's magazines. One of them is open to an article called "The Sunshine Nursery." Everything in the nursery is brilliant yellow with bows made of sparkling material. It's a room you could go blind in.

"No good at all," I say. "But maybe that's all you've got."

I hang up Melyssa's clothes and she turns the TV back on.

I keep thinking about what Ms. Miller said about people getting tired and not giving up on myself even when everyone else does. And how Pete made fun of me for being a martyr. I stare into the basket of lonely socks. I have to ask myself, am I not applying so I can help Melyssa, or so I can avoid losing?

The next night at bedtime I get the boys around. I have a hole the size of a bowling ball in my guts about dropping out of the competition. The application was all I had been thinking about—well, almost all I'd been thinking about—for so many weeks I didn't even realize how much it had been keeping me from seeing all the other stuff in my life. I need to get away.

"Where were we when last we left our pirates?"

"They just brought the girl back on the ship after tossing her for being a witch," says Carson.

"Right you are, mate. The island of Isabela lay before them, her vast volcanoes, five fire-belching mountains, rising into the sky. The island was inhabited by hosts of mythic creatures like giant tortoises with saddle backs and fist-sized birds the color of a flame, red crabs with bright blue eyes, and tiny dragons that swim. Around the island's rim, lurking in watery caves, lived one of the strangest creatures of all: the flightless cormorant."

"Like in your books," says Carson.

"Yes, but magic. And, like all things magical, dangerous.

The first thing they learned on the island was that this was going to be an expensive trip."

"Who told them that?" says Carson.

"The penguins."

"Penguins live at the South Pole, not the equator," says Brett.

"Not these penguins. These bullets of buoyancy are perfectly adapted to their home at the equator. They use the cold water that flows from the South Pole to cool their tail feathers. And they are smart too. They know a ship of suckers when they see one."

"They talk?" says Carson.

"All penguins talk. If you speak penguin."

"What did they say?" says Danny.

"The fat head honcho penguin said, 'Honk honk gasp . . . It's going to cost you one thousand doubloons to park that ship of dreams on our shore.'"

"Is that a lot?" says Carson.

"Well, not if you're the King of England. But alas these were poor pirates. No savings. No retirement. Not even enough rum to get them through another week. They didn't have any way to pay. The Deadendiers knew they had to land to get the jewel to save their town, so they volunteered to work off their debt. And the penguins took them up on their offer.

"The fat penguin said, 'When you have pulled a thousand fish from the sea, we will let you come ashore.'

"To the surprise of the crew, the pirate king agreed.

"'What are you thinking, Cap'n?' said the first mate. 'We'll be trolling the rest of our lives ta catch that many fish.'

"The pirate king nodded yes, but the wink in his eye said no. At nightfall the pirate king came to the Deadendiers and told them to draw straws. The prince cheated and won. The pirate king told him he had won the honor of swimming to shore and stealing the jewel while the rest of the crew anchored there and pretended to fish. If the prince got past the larcenous penguins, he would have to find his way to the cave of the cormorants, and get past the horrible heron, and then he must tell the cormorants a riddle that they couldn't solve. Only then would the mysterious birds release one of their precious gems to chase away the evil brain-killing trolls on Deadendia.

"The prince said, 'You want me to jump in the water at night?'

"'Yes,' said the pirate king.

"'Have you seen what salt water does to silk? My clothes will be ruined,' said the prince.

"Before the maid could hear the pirate king's profane response, she slipped into the water. She had only been swimming a few minutes when she saw large white shapes coming toward her. A white-tip reef shark, a manta ray, and a sea turtle, all swimming by the light of the silvery moon. The maid motioned to the creatures, but they swam on."

"She motioned to the shark?" says Carson. "Is she crazy?"

"Not at all. They're harmless in these waters. But one creature didn't ignore the swimmer. A bored sea lion bull body slammed the poor girl. The maid batted the animal away, but it was no use. She was soon to drown when suddenly a pod of dolphins arrived, chirping and chatting after a night at the Oceanside Café. They swam past the sea lion, providing temporary shelter. One dolphin even bumped up to the maid and offered her a fin to shore. In no time at all the girl found herself on the beach. As the sun rose over the volcanoes, she huddled wet, cold, alone, and in search of the jewel she could not even describe. It was the best morning of her life."

I stand to go, and the boys moan. I step into the hallway and nearly land on my very uncomfortable sister, crunched against the wall.

I pull her up and we walk to the kitchen.

"How's your head?" I say.

"You aren't going to start studying me like one of your sad little cormorants, are you?"

"No. But baby science is kind of cool. It's like creation in a bottle."

"Yeah, it's real cool," she says, "if you don't mind being a bottle that can't pee, walk, or wear anything but a circus tent."

"But you make the tent thing really work."

Melyssa laughs. "I hope the scullery maid gets the jewel. Eventually."

"She will. She's a scullery maid. She's used to crap happening."

# 37

# Outclimbing Escape Strategy:
## *When a smaller prey plays the angles.*

I sit in my classes and look out the window at the various views of the parking lot. Someone went to a lot of trouble to give us views of the parking lot. Maybe it was to help our young minds feel refreshed with sunshine. That's what I'd like to think. But most of the people I see sitting around me are seniors, and they don't look too refreshed. They look like they're on the downhill slide to nothing.

This is all the school they're planning, and in a few weeks we'll be officially free of learning anything at all, except a trade that's supposed to keep us from starving to death. School's out forever, followed by a drum solo.

During lunch I go to the library. At least I can read about being somewhere else.

Much to my surprise, Erik strolls in a few minutes later and plunks down next to me, like we're still big buddies. I keep my face in my book.

"I heard you dropped out."

I look up but don't say anything.

"I would have won anyway, you know."

"If you thought that, you wouldn't be here," I whisper, then I put my head back in my book.

"You know you really never wanted to go. You couldn't leave this town if your life depended on it. You were doing it to get back together with me."

I put my book down. I look Erik in the face. "Really? Please try to get over yourself. I know what you did with the complaint. You're such a weasel, you couldn't just deal with me beating you, so you tried to cheat. Like you cheat on everything. That's what you do when you can't win, Erik. You cheat."

He whispers, "Gee, Myra, I love this new side of you."

"I don't care if you love it or not." I'm not whispering.

"I don't know why you have to act like this."

"Like what?" I feel kids looking at me.

Erik tips his head forward and speaks with a distinct hiss. "I sent that complaint because you have an inappropriate relationship with Pete. I know he's been *helping* you. It's nauseating." His nose pinches together when he says this. He couldn't look any more self-righteous if he had a pulpit in front of him.

I pick up my book and stuff it in my backpack. "Strap your barf bag on then, Saint Erik. Things are going to get a little bumpy."

# 38

# Plumage:
## *Fancy feathers.*

When I get home from school, Melyssa is snoring like a blood-hound.

I sit down and replay the whole Erik thing in my head. I flip through the magazine I bought her a few days ago. It's a local outdoor magazine about places you can camp in the state with little kids. It seemed like a good idea when I bought it, something to get her thinking about the cool parts of being a mom, but now that I'm looking through it, all I can see are the pages plastered with smiling, perfect families. I wonder where Zeke is. If I knew, I'd call him and tell him to get his butt over here. She misses him, even though she says she doesn't.

And if he doesn't hurry up and get some courage, he's going to miss out on the birth of his kid. I don't know that I like Zeke, but I think he should be around for at least that.

I look at a few more pages and start reading an article about some mountain you can go to in the Uintas. With the article is a picture of a family sitting on a rock, and the mother is pointing things out to the kids like it's a classroom. The caption says, "Respect Your Mother (Earth)."

The two kids look like they're having the time of their lives. The same old clichés every vacation ad has. But when I look at the cheesy mom standing there, it makes a deep, twisting hole in my heart. Regardless of what I've experienced in my own life, I want to be that person. Even if that person doesn't exist. And I can't be her if I'm some bitter mope who walks around doing things just because she should.

I go get the boys out of their room. "Brett, I need you to keep an eye on Melyssa."

"An eye on her?"

"Call me if she asks for me. Andrew, you are in charge of making dinner. We can have macaroni and cheese with a salad. Can you handle that?"

"A salad?"

"You've seen them?"

"Yeah, but what do I put in it?"

"Use your imagination."

I sketch for a minute in the basement, raid a few closets, and then I sit down at the sewing machine in Mom's room. I put on my headphones and crank it. Sometimes you have a fairy godmother, and sometimes you have to be your own.

When Dad gets home, I tell him I need some help tonight. I have some important work to do.

"Like what?"

"I'm fixing up a dress for the Senior Dinner Dance."

"You're going? Who are you going with?"

"Pete. And I would like to look decent."

"Pete? Your boss Pete?" he says. "Isn't he a little old for this kind of thing?"

"He's not my boss. And he's going as a friend."

"Is Erik taking that other girl?"

"I don't know. How do you know about her?"

"Carson told me she's a wench."

I've always suspected that kid was a genius. "Carson's right."

"You go ahead and work, honey. I'm sure we can handle Melyssa and dinner."

"Thanks."

I pull two layers of gauze I've been saving over one side of a yellow sundress that I bought last summer, then I embroider a sunflower onto it to hold everything together. It takes a long time, because I have to do it one little stitch at a time. I get off center and have to take a bunch of stitches out, which takes a whole lot longer than putting them in. Then I cut some petals from the leftover gauze and roll the seams and tuck them into the embroidery. Eventually it takes shape. It starts to pucker and stand up. Almost like it's blooming.

Just before midnight I walk past my dad, who has gone to sleep on the couch so I could work on the machine in his room. I look up at the clock on the wall. As it strikes, I realize I'm eighteen.

I sleep until seven. I have to get Carson and Danny ready for soccer, and then take Melyssa to her obstetrician, but I'm so tired my eyebrows hurt. Maybe it's my age. I feel my arms and face. No giant wrinkles yet. But I'm ready to go to bed when I wake up. I'm an adult.

I go upstairs for a bowl of adult wheat flakes. I'm wearing an adult bathrobe. Okay, the robe says PINKY on the back, but close enough. The house is deathly quiet. The sun is coming through the curtains, making bright yellow squares on the linoleum. I wonder if my parents will remember it's my birthday. Not that I care. There are more important things to do today than worry about a messy, expensive party. Just my dad helping out last night so I could work was great.

I pour the cereal. A small piece of colored paper falls into my bowl. I recognize the artist before the artwork. A Carson crayon masterpiece. It's a picture of a girl waving a very long arm from a boat. There are gulls flying and there is a big sun in the sky. It says "Happy Birthday Skulry Maid."

No party necessary. I'm good.

The hour and a half I was going to give myself to get ready for the dance doesn't materialize. Mel's appointment takes forever. The doctor wasn't happy, but at least the baby's heartbeat is strong.

I run into the house when we get home. I have thirty minutes, and I want to look good.

I don't go all out on my makeup and hair. But I go out

a little. I don't want to look like a total waif. Not that I care what Erik thinks; I already know what Erik thinks. He thinks he won. He thinks he beat me. And in a way, maybe he did. But it doesn't mean I can't use the blush that makes me look somewhere between sweet and cheap. And it doesn't mean I can't have fun tonight.

Melyssa has a pair of yellow heels that are a half size too small and kind of sexy for my taste, but they look pretty with the dress. I stand in front of the mirror looking at my work. My dress doesn't look like a prom dress. It doesn't even come to my knees, and it's too simple. But when I go upstairs to model for Dad, he raises his eyebrows.

"How old is Pete again?" he says.

"Dad," I whine. "He's totally doing this out of pity."

Melyssa smiles for the first time in about a hundred years. "Nobody's going to feel sorry for you dressed like that, Little Sis. Man, why didn't I get your legs, Dad? I was robbed."

Mom walks into the room. She's only been home a few minutes and she looks beat. "Myra! Twirl around, dear! Look at you."

"She made it in one day," says Melyssa.

Mom says, "I couldn't make a dress like that if you gave me all month. You look as pretty as a picture."

"Yep," says Dad. "That little puke is going to be sorry."

"Oh, please," I say. "I probably won't even see Erik there."

"Well, he'll see you," says Dad. "Unless he's blindfolded and locked in a box."

As cheesy as this love fest is, it makes me feel fluttery and happy inside. And I like how I look even more because I made the dress myself.

"You guys aren't all going to come to the door, are you?"

"Wouldn't miss it," says Dad. "And I plan on cleaning my gun in the living room before he gets here too."

Mom runs to her room and brings me back her necklace with a tiny diamond. She only wears it on special occasions.

"What if I lose it?" I say.

"Put it on," she says. "You won't lose it. It's your birthday present."

I hold the necklace in my fingertips and look at my tiny mother. This is the nicest thing she owns. It's about the only nice thing she owns, unless you count her sewing machine, which I don't.

"I can't," I say. "Dad gave this to you."

Mom puts her hand out sternly, but her eyes are wet. "It's from both of us. Better put it on."

I put the delicate chain around my neck. Mom fastens it for me with her small, rough fingers. Before she steps away, she whispers, "You're growing up, my girl."

I shouldn't be surprised when Pete shows up in Chaco sandals. They don't look bad with his wrinkled, sand-colored suit. His hair is clipped short and he's trimmed his beard. He smells like vanilla soap. He's holding a wilted daisy. Just one. He looks so out of place in my parents' living room when I invite him in I almost burst out laughing.

Instead I introduce him to Dad, flanked by Mom, Carson,

and Danny. You'd think I'd never had a date in my life.

Pete puts his hand out to Dad. "It's a pleasure to meet you, Mr. Morgan."

Carson leans over to Danny. "I thought he'd be taller."

Dad gives Pete the business handshake. "Myra tells us you work at the marina."

I shudder. If Dad asks Pete about his intentions, I may have to go find that gun Dad was talking about.

"Yes, sir. It's a way to get through graduate school." He puts out his hand to my mom and brothers. Mom acts like she's in pain, but the two rats give Pete a smile. Melyssa walks in, says hi, looks prettier than I am in spite of being pregnant, gives me a wink, and walks out. Brett and Andrew waltz in on their way out to play basketball at the park. "Hey," they say in unison.

"Hey," says Pete with teenage perfect pitch.

*Hey*, I think, *has sixty seconds ever felt so long?*

We step over the Big Wheel and bikes to get to the van.

"You look phenomenal," he says. "I like your dress."

"I made it myself," I say.

"I can tell," he says.

I look up. "Really?"

"I mean, it looks like you," he says. "It's shiny." He grins, and I grin back because I'm powerless not to.

"Thanks, I think. I like your sandals."

He takes my hand, right in front of my family. "Anything for the princess."

I scramble up into his magic pumpkin van and sail off to the ball.

Because it's Senior Dinner Dance, we don't have to slump around in the dumpy gym at our school. The main event is at a hotel in the city. On the way Pete says, "Your dad looked like he had his doubts about letting you go out the door with me."

"Yeah." I run my hands through my hair before I remember Melyssa arranged it into place with some stuff in a tube. I also seem to have forgotten how to talk.

Pete smiles like he gets it. "If you were my daughter, I'd hire a sharpshooter."

We drive in silence the rest of the way into the city. I tap my hand on my thighs and wonder if I'm going to sweat on the material when we dance. Pete drums his fingers on the steering wheel to some angsty song I've never heard before.

When we pull up to the Red Lion Hotel underground parking, the tollbooth guy looks at Pete and says, "Will you two be checking in for the night?"

Pete tips his head to the man. "No, we're just here for a quickie."

The old geezer immediately peers over Pete to look at me, shrinking into my seat. "Don't make it too quick, son," he says.

That does it. The night is officially awkward.

# 39

# Sky-pointing:
*The mating dance of the blue-footed booby.*

When we walk into the dance, no one even looks up. We're late, and everyone is busy acting like they do this sort of thing all the time. The truth is, us Cyprus Pirates hit the scene in downtown Salt Lake about as much as we vacation in the Hamptons or shop on Rodeo Drive.

Pete says, "Aw, I'd forgotten."

"What?"

"How good it is to not be in high school."

I should have known better. Even to me, all these boys in dorky tuxes and girls in push-up bras are ridiculous. "You want to leave?"

Pete takes my hand and squeezes it. "No way. I showered."

We bump through people out onto the dance floor and a few kids look at me and then at Pete's beard. Some look at his hand on mine. They don't even pretend not to stare. It's like I brought a gorilla.

Pete ignores all of them and starts shaking around. He so doesn't blend. Which, oddly enough, is nice. When I stop looking at everyone else looking at him, I see a guy who has beautiful green eyes, a wrinkled suit, and dance moves I'm pretty sure he made up himself.

The band plays something slow and Pete grabs my arm. "Where I went to high school we had to be a Bible's length away during the slow stuff."

"I've never read the Bible," I say.

He steps closer to me. "So we're good then." He feels warm and familiar. "Are you having a nice time?"

I don't answer. I lean in and take a breath and I feel a hundred miles away but right where I am.

"Hey, teach!"

I look up and see Erik and Ariel dancing next to us. He has his hand on her back under her long, twisted curls. She steps gracefully with him, following everything he does. Then, almost as if I scripted it myself, she misses a step and he corrects her. He pulls on her fuchsia dress just hard enough that she looks up and frowns. He looks back at her with that flicker of frustration he used to give me. It's her fault. She wasn't keeping up.

"Hey, Erik," says Pete. "How's tricks?"

Erik smiles at Ariel, who looks certifiably gorgeous. "Never better," he says.

"Glad to hear it," says Pete.

I don't say anything.

Ariel grins with flawless teeth. "Wow, Myra, where'd you get your dress?"

It isn't a compliment.

"Isn't it incredible?" says Pete. "She made it."

"It's *perfect* for you, Myra. It even has little homemade flowers," says Erik. Each word comes off his lips with precision.

I know it's just a dress and a dumb dance, but why does he have to do this? Even in all the noise, there is silence around me. Clarity.

"You're such an ass," says Pete.

Erik stops dancing and calls back. "At least I'm not scamming on high school girls when I'm in graduate school."

Pete turns to face Erik. I step in front of Pete and move toward Erik. I stand right next to Erik and Ariel so only they can hear me. My voice is calm and clear. "Nobody is *scamming* on me. I'm not too stupid to know how sex works, Erik. I'm too smart to have it with you." His handsome face is frozen. I can feel people stopping around us.

Ariel's smile oozes condescension. She flicks her hand on Erik's back. "He dumped you, Myra. You need to get over that."

I smile back at her. "I think I just did."

Erik's face stays frozen, but our eyes connect. I don't look away. What I see is the messed-up person I used to trust more than I trusted myself—not Prince Charming and not the measure of who I am. He's how I got here, but he's my past. In that split second, it's like the whole building cracks around me so I can also see what's on the other side of the walls. The real world.

I feel Pete's hand in mine. "Birds of a feather are flocked up together," he whispers as he swirls me away. I look back long enough to see Erik staring unhappily. Then a starter for the basketball team and his equally gawky six-foot date shuffle in front of us and eclipse Erik altogether.

The band plays a painful version of "I'll Stand by You." The lead singer's voice breaks about eight times. I kind of love the song even more for that. Pete and I move together through the music and lights. He's actually a really good dancer once he stops trying to be hip. Maybe all that time in South America. I dance without trying to anticipate his steps because I don't need to and because no one can predict Pete. Then the music ends. I look up at Pete and I know it's time to go. "I'm done."

"You're done? No dinner?"

"Is that okay? I want to go someplace else now. Someplace without people."

Pete says, "I know just the place."

The tollbooth grandpa is waiting for us when we pull out. Pete says, "Her mom wants her home by ten."

"Heaven help you," the man says.

I don't ask Pete where we're going. It doesn't matter. There's a little bit of daylight left and we're going to spend it together. We head north on I-15. Pete is quiet so I roll down my window and put my arm out of the van. I weave my hand through the air. I know where we're going.

I remember our first field trip. Pete said, "There's always evolution, baby." I thought Pete was crazy then, but tonight I think I know what he meant. I breathe in the wind and sun and smell of spring. Before long we are on the winding road that leads to Egg Island.

We drive to the trailhead. Pete drags out one of his moldy blankets. He isn't talking much, especially for Pete, but I like just being with him. I walk a few steps behind him, then take off my sister's uncomfortable shoes and make my way bare-foot to the lookout rocks. The gray sand feels good between my toes.

Pete finds a dry spot on the hill, and we sit down on the blanket together, a body's length apart. I look out over the lake and listen to the grebes chattering a half mile away. I can still hear the music from the dance playing in my head, but now there are birds singing along. The sun is dropping quickly behind the mountains, and it splits and sparkles on the water.

The space between me and Pete makes everything electric inside me. I lie back and let the breeze cool my face. I like the crazy way it makes me feel to lie down next to Pete with my eyes closed, like I'm driving with my lights off.

I feel him move closer.

I keep my eyes closed. "I love it when the days get longer. Are the days always the same at the equator? I never thought to ask."

Pete's voice floats over me. "Pretty much. The sun comes up at about six and sets at about six all year."

I open my eyes and see that Pete is looking at me. I prop up on my side. "It sounds perfect."

"I don't know, Myra. I kind of think perfect is something you agree to, not something that happens." He rests his hands on his knees and looks out over the water. "People are miserable there just as much as they are anywhere else. Probably more so, because there's so much poverty. But let's not talk about the Galápagos now."

"Why not?" I say.

He gets up and walks around the grass-covered hill. His feet sweep into the wild grass like he's kicking at something. It startles me. After all that's happened tonight, I just assumed that Pete was happy too. I thought his silence in the van was because he didn't need to say anything. When he comes back, he sits down next to me and takes my hand. His skin is rough and dark compared to mine. He traces a figure eight on my hand with his finger, then gently moves his hand up my arm. I have no idea what's going on, but I know he's getting ready to tell me.

He says, "You're beautiful, you know that?" He doesn't sound happy about it.

"Thanks," I say, feeling the heat in my face. "What's wrong?"

Pete looks away. "What's wrong is what happened with Erik."

I nod. "I don't care. I had a great time anyway."

"I'm not talking about tonight."

"What do you mean?"

"How long did you two go out?"

"Too long, that's for sure."

"Why? I mean, why did you go out with him so long if he's such a big jerk?"

"He wasn't a jerk at first. At least I didn't realize it. What difference does it make?" I don't like where this is going.

"Stop it, Myra. I want you to talk to me." Pete puts his face close to mine, still holding on to my hand. "What did he do to you? I wanted to kick his ass tonight. It would be nice if you gave me a solid reason."

I pull away from him. That is the last thing I am going to talk about tonight, or ever. "I don't think it's your business. And besides, it's over."

"Is it? Because he's applying and you aren't."

I try to catch up to what this is about. "You think I dropped out for Erik?"

"Maybe not for him, but maybe because he makes you feel like you didn't have any business applying."

"I dropped out to take care of my sister."

"You could have found a way. You bailed."

I don't know where this is coming from, but it doesn't matter. I don't like being broadsided. I'm tired of guys who think they can bully me. "I didn't *bail*. I made a choice."

"But why that choice? I mean, come on, Myra. Look at

you! You ought to be against the law in that dress and you're smart as hell. Why would you quit when all you need is to get out of here?"

"Because my family needs me too."

"But what about you? You're learning to see, Myra. You see the amazing details of the world. You didn't have to go to the Galápagos to learn that. You evolved right here in your own backyard. But that's why you can't stop now. And going to Ecuador, surrounded by other students and teachers, would be the beginning of everything for you."

"I have to help Melyssa. Don't you get that?"

"That's bull. You are willing to fight for everyone who needs you, except yourself. I want to know why."

Three minutes ago I was completely happy. Pete's the one person I don't want to fight with, and he's completely pissing me off. I don't want to talk about Erik. I don't want to think about not applying. "You act like I have to go or my whole life will be ruined."

"Did he hurt you? Is that why you're scared?"

"I'm not scared." I scramble up to get away from him. "I decided to help my sister. But you wouldn't understand that. Everything is just a big adventure to you. You went off and left your family and never cared about anyone but yourself. You still don't."

Pete stays sitting. He lets air out of his lungs and then shakes his head. "That's not true, Myra." He looks at me, then looks away. I know I've hurt him, but I won't let him do this to me. I've made my choice. No one is going to control me anymore.

"Just leave," I say.

He stares at me. "Leave? Leave you here in the dark? In that dress? And those crazy little shoes?" He shakes his head. "Not a chance."

"My family will come get me."

"That'll be the day," says Pete.

I flip out my phone and start shimmying down the rocks. Pete comes after me. "You're being ridiculous."

The phone rings five times before someone picks up.

"Hello?" says Melyssa. Her voice tells me she was sleeping.

"Mel, why are you answering the phone? Can you send Dad to get me?"

"I thought you went to the dance. Are you okay? Why are you breathing so hard?"

"I'm perfectly fine," I say. I talk loud so Pete will hear. "I'll be at the tollbooth entrance to Antelope State Park."

"Antelope Island? Alone? What's going on?"

"I'm fine. Really. I'll be at the entrance. Thanks, Mel." I hang up my phone. I turn to Pete, who is right behind me, "They're on their way."

"I'm not leaving you here in the dark."

I still have Mel's shoes in my hand. It's a nice night. The moon is out. I start walking. I figure it will take about as long to get to the tollboth as it will for my dad to exceed the speed limit to get here. The blood is pumping so hard in my brain I nearly forget that Pete is still behind me.

He whistles to remind me.

I don't turn around. "They'll tow your van if you leave it here."

"Why are you doing this?"

"Because I feel like it. I'm an adult now. I get to do things without a chaperone."

I keep walking. Pete isn't whistling. After a few minutes I turn around and he's gone. When he passes me on the causeway I don't look up.

# 40

## Altricial:
### *Naked, blind, and helpless at hatching.*

When I get to the tollbooth the ranger is closing up for the night. He gives me a look like I've lost my mind. I ignore him and keep walking until I see Pete's crummy old van parked on the other side of the road. For the ranger's benefit I wave. He waves back. I don't cross the street.

There is no sign of Dad. I pull out my phone. No signal. Perfect. I move over to the side of the road and lean against the fence. Even if I have to sit here until the sun comes up, I'm not getting in that van with Peter Tree.

After a painful ten minutes or so I see the Suburban. I can tell by the way Moby is coming toward me in the dark that it's not my mother or my dad at the wheel. Only one person in my family drives that badly. And it makes me sick. How could she?

I wave and she flips the car around to the gravel shoulder.

I go over to the driver's side and open the door. "What are you doing?" I say. "Where's Dad?"

"Are you okay?" she says. "Where's Pete?"

"I'm fine. Why are you driving?"

Her face is ghostly, but she laughs softly as she slides over to the passenger side. Thank goodness for the bench seating. She says, "Right before you called, Mrs. Bridgestone discovered that Danny had turned on their hose and flooded their yard. Can you believe it? Dad had just left to do damage control. Mom's at work. I didn't want you stranded here. Some creep might grab you."

"I would have waited until Dad got home."

"You're welcome, idiot."

I look up in time to see Pete's van driving away.

All the things I've read about preeclampsia fill my head at once. It can be deadly for the mom and the baby. It can cause birth defects. It can come on like a freight train and you can't stop it. But she's here, rude and laughing, so I try not to completely freak out. Maybe her case isn't as bad as what they describe in the books. Maybe the doctors are just being cautious. Maybe the worst part of this is that my parents are going to kill me.

I step up on the running board to sit down in the driver's seat. I look down at the seat. My stomach drops. Maybe it's worse than I thought. "Melyssa," I say.

"What?" She's tipped over a little so I can't see her face. "I'm fine," she says, but her voice is brittle.

"Show me your backside."

She doesn't stop hunching over. "That's pretty personal."

"Look," I say.

Without straightening up she twists to look at the red smear on the upholstery. "What's that?"

Before I can answer she yells and jackknifes forward, hitting her head against the glove box.

"Melyssa!"

I jump into the car, willing myself to sit on top of the blood-stained seat. *Germs not important. Premature baby important.*

I say, "There's a hospital up the road. You can't have the baby until we get you to the hospital. I'm serious."

She lets out a high piercing cry, like an animal would make.

I put my face down where I can see hers. "What's happening?"

She shouts into the floor of the car. "It feels like somebody's stabbing me in the stomach, that's what's happening."

I look behind me and pull out onto the road. Traffic is light but slow. I pull onto the soft shoulder and pass three cars on the right. A car honks. I pull back onto the pavement and have a clear road. "Just give me ten minutes. I'll get you there."

Melyssa shouts, "I'm not having this baby yet!"

"Fine with me. Just wait until we get to the hospital."

I see the route to the hospital in my head. If I can get her inside, they'll know how to stop the bleeding. Maybe they can even stop her from going into labor. "Does your head hurt?"

She breathes heavily. "I just smacked it into the dashboard."

"Before. Did you have a headache before?"

She sits up but clamps back down with pain. "Three days."

I speak calmly, even though I want to kill her myself. "You've had a headache for three days and you didn't tell me?"

She groans. "*Do not* lecture me right now!"

A man pulls in front of me and I have to brake hard not to hit him. The last thing we need right now is an accident, especially since I don't think I'm getting my writhing sister into a seat belt. I have to stay in the middle of this thing. Focus on what's happening. Keep everything calm. Not think about the blood on the seats and the blood on my sister.

Melyssa says, "Oh, no way. I think I just peed all over myself."

I look away from the road quickly and see red fluid on the floor, the seat, her clothes, and speckled on my arm. It's like someone knocked over a Super Big Gulp of fruit punch, except it's sticky and it smells like stale salt water.

I concentrate on my driving so the stench doesn't drive me off the road. I think about finding the emergency room. When she's in the hospital I can clean this all up. I can take Moby to a car wash and they'll make it like it never happened.

"I'm dying," says Melyssa. She doesn't yell this, so I know she believes it.

"No, you aren't," I say. "Your water just broke. You're going to be fine." I don't tell her that it's her baby that's in trouble now.

She breathes hard, probably because she's having a contraction, then she sits up. "What does that mean? Is it bad if my water breaks?"

"It means you have to have the baby now."

She groans and twists in her seat.

"We're close. I can see the roof of the hospital."

"What?" says Melyssa. She leans back and closes her eyes with her head against the door. I switch on the child safety locks. As if this is going to help. I turn into the parking lot. She jolts again and lets out a scream. Her eyes fly open. "Ah, ah," she says. She grabs at the seat. "Myra?" She looks at me and grabs my arm so hard I nearly swerve. Everything in her face is pain. "Make it stop."

I look around and realize I'm on the wrong side of the hospital. "We're almost there. It's going to stop. We'll find someone. You're going to make it. You and the baby are both going to make it. You were born to do this."

"You'll stay with me?" she says.

"You couldn't pry me away."

"People have babies early, right?" she says.

"Every day. You're going to be just fine." I don't mention that at twenty-nine weeks the baby's lungs aren't developed fully and the chances for birth defects are still in the probable zone.

"Okay."

"Breathe," I say. "Come on. You can do this."

"I can't!" screams Melyssa.

"Breathe. In and out. Just like you practiced."

"I can't!"

"You have to," I say back, sharp as a knife.

"I know!" she yells. Then she grunts loudly. I know she's bearing down. There are three cars in front of me moving impossibly slow while they look for parking. What, is there like a discount for emergency room visits today? I honk and the man in front of me flips me off.

Melyssa grunts again, her eyes closed, lost in a tunnel of pain I can only imagine. Then she opens her eyes. "Are we there?"

"We're close."

She groans again. "Oh my holy hell, Myra, it's coming. Right now. I can't stop it. "

"Yes, you can."

"Help me!" she yells.

We're a hundred yards from the emergency entrance, but I have two cars in front of me. I turn off the engine in the middle of the parking lot and throw on the hazards. The car behind me honks. I jump out of Moby and yell at the woman behind me. "My sister's having a baby! Get a doctor out here!"

Then I fly to the passenger side and throw open the door. Warm brackish air from Melyssa's body covers me. *Germs not important. Sister important.* I climb up onto the running board and turn her to face me. "Slide back," I say. She is pushing hard. I help her back against the seat and I climb in between her legs and wedge the door shut behind me. Good thing she's wearing the hideous tent dress.

"Erggg!" she yells.

"I'm going to have to take some of your clothes off," I say. "Don't worry, I won't look."

"Like I care!" screams Melyssa.

I wiggle to her side so I can help her scoot out of her

underwear, but everything is so covered in blood, and we're wedged in so tight it's like the clothes are glued on. I remember the knife in my first-aid kit in the glove box. I grab it out and flip it open. I say, "This is for your clothes, not you."

She's crying. "Don't leave!"

"Are you kidding?"

She smacks the seat with her forearm. "I mean it."

I begin cutting her clothes. In any other moment of my life, the germs and blood in these two feet of space would paralyze me. But I'm dead calm. Just as I pull the clothes away, a baby, a terribly small, perfectly formed baby, comes from my sister's legs in a wave of blood and water. The baby's delicate body is purple and gray and is covered in white film. I catch her and tip her sideways like I saw online. Except there were doctors and they weren't doing it in a Suburban. I take my red hands and lift her to me, but she's still connected to my sister's womb by a twisty cord the size of a pen, so I lean forward to be close.

Her body is warm, floppy, and about the size of an overgrown eggplant. But the precision of each unbearably small feature is so perfect, so full of what it's becoming, that she's unlike anything I have every imagined. She is divine.

I think my head is going to explode. I touch her back with my finger. She doesn't respond. And yet I know she is alive. She fills every particle around her with life.

"It's a girl," I say quietly.

Melyssa yells, "Is she okay?"

I lift my thin, yellow dress around her to keep her warm, trying to think what I should do next.

*Where are those doctors?*

"Let me warm her up," I say. I tear the gauze from my dress and tuck her into it.

"Is she all right? Hold her up so I can see her."

"Let me warm her up."

Melyssa lifts her head to see us. "Okay. Get her warm."

Behind me the door opens and sucks all the air out of the Suburban. Someone grabs my shoulder. "Miss! Miss! I'm a doctor. I need you to give me the baby."

I turn my head and see a middle-aged woman in bright green scrubs with a dozen other people behind her. It's so cold outside I turn my back on them to stop the draft. I draw the little purple body to me. "Breathe, honey, breathe."

"Where are you going?" says Melyssa.

"I'm giving her to the doctor," I say.

I slide out of the doctor's way. She's holding a small blanket that she wraps around the baby. A second doctor comes up behind her with instruments. I push around the other staff and get into the backseat where I can hold Melyssa's hand. "Doing great, Mel," I say.

The second doctor doesn't look happy. "Come on," he says to the first doctor.

The first doctor puts the baby closer to Melyssa and the second doctor clamps off the umbilical cord and snips it.

The first doctor looks at the baby and then at the other doctor. There's a little wrinkle in the baby's forehead and a cry so faint it could be my imagination, except the man yells, "Go!"

Then the first doctor is running with another team of people in scrubs who are running to meet her and my sister is saying, "Where is she? Is she breathing? Myra! Myra!"

"She's breathing."

The doctor says, "You need to get out of this car and onto the stretcher. We need to get you inside too."

He gets out of the car and stands there waiting for her like she's just going to bounce off the seat onto the stretcher.

Mel looks up at me. Her eyes aren't right. "Where is she?" she says.

"They took her into the hospital. She's going to be fine," I say.

"The baby needs oxygen," says the man, looking at me. "And this woman needs a surgeon before she bleeds to death." He calls to his staff. "Pull her out."

Two men in scrubs get on both ends of Melyssa and lift her onto the stretcher. Once she's on her back, I grab her hand and squeeze it.

The doctor pushes at my hand. "We have to go. You need to check her in."

The stretcher starts moving. "Is she okay?" calls Melyssa.

I run alongside. "She's perfect."

"Don't leave, Myra," she says.

"I won't."

# 41

# Hatchling:
*A new bird.*

My mom faints when she sees me. One look and . . . Bam! I guess it's the sight of me in an emergency room wearing a blood-covered sundress. Luckily, Dad grabs her quick enough that she doesn't split her head open on the chair next to her.

She comes right out of it, so nobody puts her on a stretcher or anything. And she's mad as she can be by the time she's on her feet.

"What happened?" she says.

"When?" I'm not being sarcastic. It's just that a lot of bad stuff has happened since I saw Mom last.

Dad says, "Why is there blood all over you?"

"I delivered the baby. Or at least I was there when she arrived. The blood got all over everything, including the car. The upholstery is a total mess."

"I don't care about the upholstery," says Dad.

Mom says, "What was Melyssa doing driving the car?"

"She was coming to get me."

Mom says, "I gathered that from Andrew. Why did you ask her to? You know she shouldn't drive."

"I told her to send Dad. I didn't know she was coming, and when I did, she was already there."

"Where are they now?" says Dad.

"They took them separately and told me to wait. Melyssa looked pretty good, but the baby was really small and purple. She wasn't making much noise."

Dad grabs my mom's shoulder, just to make sure she doesn't try to face-plant again.

She says, "Purple?"

"Kind of."

"How long did it take for her to start breathing?" says Dad.

"She could have been breathing at the very first. But it took a few seconds to get her to cry."

"Brain damage. Here we go," says Mom. Her face is retracting in pain. I really hope she doesn't faint again.

"We aren't going anywhere," says Dad. "Dear, for once in your life could you imagine the best thing happening? Maybe they'll both be fine. Hospitals do amazing things these days. Now let's sit."

I sit.

"Except you, Myra," says Dad. "You go buy something to wear in the gift shop." Dad cracks open his wallet and hands me eighty dollars. My dad has never volunteered that much cash to me in his life, especially not for shopping. "Get something cheerful. We want to look ready when we meet the newest member of this family."

"Thanks, Dad," I say. "But I promised Melyssa I wouldn't leave."

Mom shakes her head. "You were supposed to keep her out of trouble."

"That's not fair and you know it, Marci. Melyssa is a grown woman. She did something reckless. That isn't Myra's responsibility." Mom looks at Dad in total surprise. He looks back at her with sad frustration and then at me. "I'll call you on your cell phone if we hear anything, Myra. You can't stand here like that, you're scaring the other people in the waiting room."

On the way to the gift shop I get lost. Too much has happened for me to think clearly. I wander around the hospital entrance, trying to follow the gift shop signs with thin little arrows, but everyone gets so bug-eyed when they see me that I turn down a side hallway just to get away.

Before I know it I find myself looking into a room that looks suspiciously like a mini church. At least I think that's what the cross and the weird lighting are all about. Why people would find that crucifix stuff soothing is beyond me. But the room's empty so I go in.

I sit on the little bench they have just for this occasion. There is soft, morbid organ music playing. I know the whole room is designed to make you feel like someone or something out there in the universe cares about your problems, but all it does is make me sad. I think of all the other people who have been on this bench and I wonder how things turned out for them. Which is weird in a way, because if I'm thinking about those people's problems now, then after the fact, someone is, or was going to be, out there worrying about them. I giggle. Clearly I'm in massive post-trauma denial mode.

Maybe things are worse than I thought. And maybe they aren't.

But that's the thing about me. I can't accept that things are going to turn out badly for Melyssa. I just know they aren't. It's not even that I feel optimistic. I just know she's going to be all right. I'm not so sure about the baby, because I don't know the baby. But I think the baby will make it too.

And then what will happen? As selfish as it sounds, I ask myself, what is going to happen to me now? And then I know, as quickly as I ask myself the question. I know that Melyssa will find her way, but that I don't want to be like her. I felt that amazing little baby come into my arms and I knew at that surreally beautiful moment that I wanted something else. The baby is here. Melyssa is going to be all right. And it's my turn to have a life.

I look at the cross again. If there is a God, he/she/it can't like that thing. If it means what I think it does, it's all about death. Doesn't the world, with all its elaborate plants and animals and perverted little microbes seem to be more about life than death?

I close my eyes so I won't have to look at anything else, and I think, *We could use some help.*

Of course nothing happens. Except that closing my eyes

makes me realize that I'm exhausted and I never want to open them again.

But first I have to find that stupid gift shop so I can stop looking like a stabbing victim.

I step into the hallway and look for the signs. Soon I'm back to the hospital entrance. And do you know who I find there?

I find Zeke, yelling at an admitting nurse. I recognize him instantly by his wrestling stance. But I'm thrown off by his clothes. He's wearing a pair of nice black pants and a starched shirt, like a waiter. His hair is combed back and he's shaved. In spite of the fact that he's yelling, he looks good. Zeke looks like he has a job.

Zeke must feel me staring. He turns around and gets a load of my bloody dress, and he goes white as the wall behind him. And then . . . Bam! Good thing that nurse knows how to catch. I've seen enough blood for one day.

After reviving Zeke and sending him off to find my parents, I buy a lilac sweat suit. It's about the same color as the baby. The woman in the pink smock at the counter says, "Looks like you had an accident."

"You have to watch those ketchup bottles in the cafeteria."

She avoids touching me when she gives me my change.

I walk into the bathroom and come out a normal person. I stuff the evidence of my evening in the trash can. Suddenly my phone goes off.

"How are they?" I say.

"Melyssa feels good enough to cuss her doctors. They're asking that you head up to neonatal on the seventh floor right away."

"And what about the baby?"

"That's going to take some time to figure out."

I walk as quickly as I can to the elevator. I wish Pete was here. I'm in the mood for the Galápagos cheer.

> You might as well step back,
> Uh-huh.
> You might as well step back.

# 42

# Field of View:
*What you see in your scope.*

A week after the application deadline I go to see Pete at the pier. He's not there. Ranger Bobbie is covering while he's at school. "He's getting that dang trip set up."

"Oh," I say lightly. "Have they picked who's going to go yet?"

"I think so."

"They have?"

"Well, at least I think so," says Bobbie. "I think Pete said that the comedian and the jerk won. He didn't see any of the entries, but he said the twins' drafts were pretty bad."

"Oh," I say. I feel the blood rushing to my face. I have to leave.

"You okay, honey? You look a little pale."

"No . . . I'm fine."

"I know it's tough on you. You'd a won for sure if you had entered. But the bright side is maybe I can talk you into coming back to work here. I'm getting sick of things growing on that desk again, and I'm not talking about flowers either."

"I'd like that," I say. At least I think I say it. My brain feels like a Russian nesting doll, buried in layers of conversations with myself.

"Yeah, so would I," says Bobbie. "How's your sister and her miracle baby doing?"

"Good. Really well," I say.

My cell rings. Dad's voice shouts through the speaker. "Myra. Are you somewhere where you can see a TV?"

I try to focus. "I'm at the marina. What's going on?"

"Turn on channel seven. Fast."

I fumble to turn on the clubhouse TV only to see the last ten seconds of my one day as a chicken immortalized on the small screen. I'm being mugged on national TV. At least I'm covered by the costume.

Ranger Bobbie cracks up. Then my chicken head comes off. Ranger Bobbie stops laughing. "Myra, is that you?"

They replay the tackle scene over and over. They do it slower each time and the audience laughs harder.

"Oh," says the announcer. "Talk about a drive-through."

"That's awful," says Bobbie, and then spurts out another laugh.

The announcer interviewing Jonathon the fink says, "How did you get this on film?"

"An artist never reveals his sources," says Jonathon. "But if you're out there, Myra, you look great in feathers!"

On another day I might think this was funny, but I'm way past not in the mood. I whisper, "I'm going to kill that kid with my bare hands." I mean it. Jonathon is a dead man.

The TV guy says, "And there you have it, 'Chicken Sandwich.'"

I sit through two more videos of people being humiliated. I am too mad to move.

The man on the TV finally says, "So viewers, which will it be? 'Tommy Goes Tinkle,' 'Udder Madness,' or 'Chicken Sandwich?'"

Ranger Bobbie says, "Sorry, Myra, nothing's as funny as a kid peeing off the balcony onto his sister! You're going down."

"Like I want to win!"

"And the winner is . . . drumroll please . . . for ten thousand dollars . . . 'Chicken Sandwich!'"

The camera pans to Jonathon. He's waving his hands in the air as the confetti falls on him. His beady little eyes shine. He's delighted with himself. Of course he is. The little toad just made ten thousand dollars off me.

The announcer puts the mike in his face. "What are you going to do with the money?"

"I think I'll buy a new camera," he says. "Then move to California."

"What about your friend?" says the announcer. "Does she get some money too?"

Jonathon looks at the man. "Yeah, yeah. I guess. If she goes out with me."

"That's the spirit, my boy. Watch her get pummeled and then bribe her with money. Believe me, it works like a charm." The announcer rolls his eyes at the audience.

I put my head back on the couch while my phone rings. I press Ignore and it rings again. I turn it off.

# 43

## Flash:

*A small lake or pond caused by rain.*

Dad throws the door open for me. "He's already called!"

"Who's called?" I say.

"Jonathon!"

There's a short list of people I would like to call me. Jonathon isn't one of them. "That was fast," I say. "Did he leave an address where I can send my pipe bomb?"

Melyssa is slouching over her donut in a rare appearance. Between pumping milk, hanging out with Zeke, and being at the hospital learning how to take care of the still unnamed bambina, she isn't home much. "You'd better hear the rest of what Dad has to say before you kill him."

"Let me guess, he wants to pay me fifty bucks so I won't sue him."

Andrew says, "It's a little better than that."

"He wants to give you a thousand," says Brett.

"You should sue for half if you ask me," says Melyssa. "You're the talent."

"He wants to give me a thousand dollars?"

"When did you work at Chicken Little?" says Dad.

Mom says, "I wish he'd won in time for your contest, honey. I'm sorry."

"You are?"

"Yes, I am," she says. "I mean it. I was wrong, Myra. You'd have won."

"Of course you would have," says Dad.

"Of course you would have," says Melyssa. "And you can still apply for all kinds of things. You're a science freak now. You're like Diane Fossey, Rachel Carson, and Julia Child all mixed up in one. Science Barbie, but with the brain included."

I look at my parents. "You'd have wanted me to go?"

Mom grabs my shoulders and hugs me. Really hugs me. "I read your proposal. Melyssa showed me. It's wonderful. I'm so sorry you missed your deadline."

It does me in. I burst like one of Brett's superdeluxe, heinous water balloons. I bawl like a big fat baby. My shoulders shudder. I wheeze. When I can get myself upright again, I say to my entire speechless family, "I didn't miss the deadline. I got a credit card advance, filled up my bank account, and entered my proposal without telling anyone."

"You entered the contest without telling us?" says Dad.

"Yes. I did. And I lost."

~~~~~~~

When I wake up it's dark. I can't believe I fell asleep. Upstairs I hear the TV, and Melyssa talking. She must be home from the hospital. I hear Zeke's voice too. I look through the window of my dungeon and wonder how I will face my family. I look up at the plastic stars on my ceiling and think of my first night in the basement. How scared and mad I was. How I thought my life was over because of Erik. I think of how many nights I've spent in this place, reading and falling in love with science and the natural world, and all the voices in it. It hits me that somehow, while I have been lying here on my sleeping bag in my parents' basement, reading by the light of my crummy lamp, the world has become a bigger place for me. Even without a ticket to see it in person.

Maybe I really have evolved. I hope that doesn't mean I'm going to have to give up ironed money.

There's a knock at the top of the stairs. The door creaks open. "Hello down there!" yells Mom. "Can you come up? The phone's for you."

I rub my face. Who would it be? The possibilities don't do much for me. "Can you take a message?"

"I think you'd better come get it, honey."

When I get to the top of the stairs my mom has a funny-sad look on her face. My dad is worse. "Is the baby okay?"

"The baby is fine," Mom says, and hands me the phone.

"Hello, is this Miss Myra Morgan?" The voice on the other end is loud and dramatic, like an old-fashioned radio announcer.

"Yes."

"Well, good. I've just had a nice chat with your parents. Wonderful people. You must be very proud of them."

"Yes," I say cautiously. The look on Dad's face as I talk is giving me an instant bellyache.

"Well, this is Kenneth Whitehead. I'm the man who funds the scholarship program you applied for. You may have heard of me."

"Yes, I have."

"Well, good. Good. I have called to extend an invitation for you to attend the university's expedition to the Galápagos Islands. Would you be interested?"

I push the air up from my stomach but nothing comes. I can't breathe.

"Miss Morgan, are you there?"

I say out loud, "I thought Pritchett and Erik won."

"Oh, yes, Pritchett Danning did win. And he's accepted. But you are our other winner."

"Not Erik Christenson? Are you sure?"

"Quite sure."

"I don't believe it."

"Well, I'd be the person to believe I think. Actually, you wrote the highest-ranking essay. Congratulations."

"Me? Me. Not Erik Christenson?"

"Off the record, Ms. Morgan, Mr. Christenson's essay was disqualified."

"Disqualified? Like for plagairism or something? How would he even do that on a proposal?"

"I've think I've said enough already, don't you?"

I suddenly have this vision of Pete's dad as the actor who played the Wizard of Oz, after he comes out from behind the curtain. He really shouldn't have told me about Erik. I'm sure there's some big rule somewhere about that. But maybe Pete isn't the only person in his family who doesn't believe in rules.

He says, "You are good at guessing, though. I think that's an important quality in a scientist."

The breath is coming back into my lungs. "Wow."

"Yes. Indeed. Now let's talk about you. I spoke with your parents and they said you have prepared your percentage of the tuition. Earned it all yourself, did you?"

I see a brief flash of myself being tackled on national TV. "The hard way."

"Wonderful. Wonderful. Builds character. I look forward to meeting you. Always love meeting a brave new mind."

I have a brave new mind. For a brave new world.

# 44

## Accommodation:
*How an animal's eyes adjust to distance by controlling light.*

Sunday after dinner I am in the basement telling a story to the boys. "Arr . . . There she stood. In the cave of the cormorants, squawking and grunting. Her riddle was told with plenty o' flapping and flipping. Says she, 'What breaks but can never be held? Has a light that can't be dispelled? Whose journey cannot be withheld?'"

Andrew and Brett pretend that they aren't trying to figure out the answer.

"I don't get it," says Carson.

"They didn't either," I say.

"'You win,' grunted the head cormorant. 'You win the jewel.'

"'Great,' said the scullery maid. 'Where is it?'

"One of the cormorants waddled forward and flapped her feathers. 'It is I,' she said.

"'It is you?' said the girl.

"'No, it is my eye,' said the bird. 'The jewel of Isabela is our eyes. We see stuff the other birds miss. It makes it so we can live on this little island and not turn into dodo birds.'"

"They're extinct, you know," says Carson.

"We know," says Andrew.

"So the girl picked up the bird. 'Do you think you will mind coming to live with me? I mean, things will be really different.'

"The bird grunted, 'If nothing ever changed, we'd all die of boredom.'

"So the girl and the cormorant went back to Deadendia with the pirates. The maid definitely did not marry the prince. But with the help of her valiant bird, the trolls were routed, air quality was improved, and the people lived happily, for a really long time. The end."

"Cool story," Brett says. "What's the answer to the riddle?"

"Oh, that's easy. The day."

Melyssa stands at the bottom of the stairs. "Hey, crew, can I interrupt? I—I mean, Zeke and I—have an announcement to make." My parents are standing behind Zeke on the stairs.

I say, "I might need to pull out another sleeping bag."

"We've decided on a name for the baby," says Melyssa.

I say, "It's about time, the poor kid."

"We want to name her Isabela."

I refuse to blubber on cue.

"But we're going to call her Egg," says Zeke to me. "After you."

I feel the traitorous salt water coming to my face. "My name isn't Egg."

Melyssa smiles. "I know, but if we name her Science Barbie she'll grow up demented and have a well-researched eating disorder."

I look around my dungeon. My family's faces glow in the light of the lamp and the shadows of the junk that has filled our lives. One thought sails brilliantly through my brain. I'm going. I'm going to the Galápagos Islands.

*You might as well step back.*

# 45

# Relict Species:

*Birds that stink at change.*

I know Erik's truck long before we pass it on the road to the marina. He's alone and driving fast. I have no idea where he would be going this time of the morning. When we make eye contact I hesitate and then I wave. He looks back at the road. It's fine. If I were him I'm not sure I'd wave either. But I'm not him. In my mirror I watch the road between us grow, and then he turns onto Main Street and he's gone.

# 46

# Fledgling:
## *A bird ready to leave the nest.*

The thing about Pete is that when he sails into the marina he could be Jason of the Argonauts. He is tan and scrappy and looks like he owns the wind.

I watch him from the marina office pavilion wondering if he will talk to me. I tried to call him three times yesterday, but I could never finish dialing. I just couldn't find any words for what I needed to say.

He sails around the dock and angles himself in. That's a tough trick with one person, but Pete is good at tricks.

I look across the sparkling water and I don't want to go anywhere without Pete. I'm just getting to know him, but I feel like I have known him my whole life. Just seeing him makes everything feel brighter. He makes me feel worthwhile. But I remember when Erik made me feel that way, and I know that I have to learn to make myself feel worthwhile. I have to learn to be happy on my own.

Pete ties up his boat and walks toward me without smiling. "What's up?"

I wait until he is close. "Hey."

"Hey," he says.

We stand there looking at each other. Maybe I should have called.

Suddenly the old guy, the one who told me I was too young to work here, bursts out of the marina office. "Pete, you are still all out of towels in the bathroom. What does it take to get towels in a bathroom these days?"

"Hey, Mack," Pete says lightly. "I'll get to it. But right now I'm talking to a woman."

Mack looks at me. "Who's this?"

"No one you know."

Mack shrugs and puts out his hand, like he's never seen me before. "Stay away from this guy. He's a troublemaker."

"I've heard that," I say.

Mack strolls back into the marina office. I smile at Pete. How can I do anything else? "Thanks for calling me a woman."

"Thanks for being one," he says.

The wind picks up and throws my hair in my face. The more I try to smooth it down, the more it flies. I give up and accept that I'm going to look like a fury. I say, "Bobbie told me that the comedian and the jerk won the scholarship."

He nods. "They did."

"I'm sorry I was a jerk," I say.

"I'm sorry I lit into you." He takes me by the shoulders,

his mouth lifting at the corners, his voice low. "I read your proposal. You have a good mind, Myra. A very good mind."

"Thanks. I'm going to keep it."

"No. You're going to grow it. I can hardly wait to talk to you when you get back."

"Will you be here when I get back?"

Pete smiles. "I'll be here."

"Hey, Pete," yells a guy from a boat tied to the dock. "You gonna kiss her or what?"

Pete and I both look at our audience. The men have dark tans, bad hair, and worse tank tops. They already have their cooler open. "Pirates," I say.

"Aye," says Pete.

Then, in front of a galley of drunk boaters, Pete puts his arms around me and looks into my eyes. I don't look away. He cocks his head to one side, waiting. "Are you sure this is okay?"

Somebody actually has a cowbell on the boat. "Are you?"

I lean in and press my lips to his. He kisses me back, gently, but pulls me close. I touch his neck with my hands and then wrap my arms around his shoulders. We fit together, but not perfectly. He pulls away and then kisses me again. Longer, and better this time. The pirates hit the ship horn and scream bloody murder. We lean away from each other just enough to get them to lay off the horn.

Pete says, "Uh, yeah. I'll be here."

Overhead the gulls call to each other, soaring and diving. I breathe in the salt of the lake in Pete's clothes and on his dark skin. I let myself relax in the imperfect space that we share. I feel myself begin to tilt and spin and disappear in the warmth of his safe arms. But I don't. I stay on my feet, ready to fly.